OUR 80TH ANNIVERSARY YEAR!

September-October 2003

ISSN 0898-5073

Cover by Jason Van Hollander

Weird Tales® is published 4 times a year by DNA Publications, Inc., & Wildside Press, in association with Terminus Publishing Co., Inc. Postmaster and others: send all changes of address and other subscription matters to DNA Publications, Inc., PO Box 2988, Radford VA 24143–2988. Single copies, $5.95 in U.S.A. & possessions; $7.00 by mail to Canada, $10.00 by first class mail elsewhere. Subscriptions: 4 issues (one year) $16.00 in U.S.A. & possessions; $22.00 in Canada, $40.00 elsewhere, in U.S. funds. Editorial matters should be addressed to Terminus Publishing Co., Inc., 123 Crooked Lane, King of Prussia PA 19406–2570. Publisher is not responsible for loss of manuscripts in publisher's hands or in transit; please see page 6 for more details. Copyright © 2003 by Terminus Publishing Co., Inc.; all rights reserved; reproduction prohibited without prior permission.

Typeset & printed in the United States of America.
Weird Tales® is a registered trademark owned by Weird Tales, Limited.

THE EYRIE

Is Sword & Sorcery still possible?

This may seem like an obvious question with an even more obvious answer. There are any number of books in the stores these days with sword-wielding heroes (and heroines) on the covers. Until a couple years ago, Randy Dannenfelser published a magazine called *Adventures in Sword and Sorcery,* to which half of the *Weird Tales*® editorial "We" (Darrell) contributed twice. (There was a Sekenre the Sorcerer story in issue #7.) Recently, we were pleased to learn that the complete Conan series of Robert E. Howard (and no one else!) is to be published in a Conan fan's dream edition by the British specialty press, Wandering Star: beautifully made hardcover editions containing only the original Howard texts, with superlative artwork. The even better news is that Del Rey books apparently plans to do a three-volume purist's-text edition of Conan, to be published in trade paperback.

What that means is that the *real* Conan the Cimmerian (who first saw the light of day in the pages of *Weird Tales* in 1932) will be available to the general, casual reading-public for the first time since . . . how long ago were those Ace paperbacks? The 1980s. It's been almost a generation then, since the actual Howard Conan stories have been generally available.

And while some sword & sorcery series seem to have faded into obscurity (we don't hear much about Brak, Thongor, or Kothar these days), certainly there has been no diminishment of interest in Michael Moorcock's variously-incarnated Eternal Champion. White Wolf did a splendid hardcover edition of Fritz Leiber's Fafhrd and the Gray Mouser not all that long ago, though a mass-market paperback of the series would be welcome about now.

But what about the state of sword & sorcery today?

Our Editorial Horde has certainly had much to do over the years with what Sprague de Camp used to call the "sacred genre." George's fanzine *Amra,* devoted to Howard, Conan, and all things swordly and sorcerous, won two Hugo awards and ran for many years. Darrell's *We Are All Legends* (Donning, 1981; presently in print from Wildside Press) is definitely sword & sorcery, by virtue of two of its episodes having first appeared in Andrew Offutt's *Swords against Darkness* anthologies. Darrell's first novel, *The White Isle,* is replete with a tragic/heroic swordsman hero, wizards, demons, an epic descent into the underworld, and — yes — even an enchanted sword, since the hero comes from the sort of family that usually has an enchanted sword or two as an heirloom.

So, what is the question?

Actually, there are two. The first is what we mean by sword & sorcery anyway. The second is whether or not this form is still viable. These seem reasonable points to bring up in the very magazine where the "sacred genre" was more or less born.

In the broadest sense, a sword & sorcery story is one about

heroic adventures, in a primitive or imaginary-world setting, with supernatural elements. Like all literary definitions, this one seems quite pat, but it gets a little vague around the edges when you examine it closely. How about stories set in the historical or quasi-historical past? What about the entire Arthurian mythos? Is *The Once and Future King* sword & sorcery? How about a story, like Poul Anderson's *The Broken Sword,* which is set in England and Scandinavia during the Viking era — save that a great deal of the action takes place in Elfland? Certainly that is considered to be a classic of sword & sorcery, sufficient to get Poul enrolled in that most exclusive of literary organizations, S.A.G.A., otherwise known as the **S**wordsmen **a**nd **S**orcerers **G**uild of **A**merica.

Our definition of sword & sorcery is paradoxically both too general and too specific. It certainly fits *The Lord of the Rings* (who says the heroic, sword-wielding hero has to be *tall?*), all its imitators and successors, i.e. the entire modern field of fantasy, all those bug-crusher trilogies, tetrologies, etc. One editor, from a firm which has made a great deal of money off what British critics have dubbed Big Commercial Fantasy, is alleged to have remarked, "Only fantasy is commercial. Everything else, including mainstream, is cult fiction."

But still we ask: is there even *such a thing* as sword & sorcery anymore, or has it evolved into something else? Arguably it has.

We come back to Robert E. Howard and Conan. The Conan series is the archetype: the heroic, grim, ruthless but honorable barbarian smiting and hewing his way across the decadent Hyborian Age, slaughtering its baleful wizards and braving the eldritch horrors which (more often than not) haunt its Cyclopean ruins.

Back around 1970, there were hordes and hoards of such books on the shelves, their covers featuring (usually) scantily-clad and (almost always) muscular heroes smiting and hewing. The look was as stereotyped as the "gothics" of the same period, those books which inevitably had a lady in trailing nightgown on the cover, fleeing from a dark (and quite possibly phallic) tower with one light aglow in the window. Research indicated that if there was *no light in the window,* the book sold less well. We wonder: would a sword & sorcery book have sold less well if the hero wielded a spear or axe, or if he wore more clothes?

STAFF:
Publishers: Warren Lapine & Angela Kessler, and John Betancourt
Editors: George H. Scithers & Darrell Schweitzer
Managing Editor: Carol Adams. Art Editor: Diane Weinstein; Assistant Editors: Kyle Phillips, Robert Waters, Joseph McCabe, Tim W. Burke, Bradley Sands, & Myke Cole. Computer Consultants: David J. Williams III & John Betancourt. Typesetting: John Gregory Betancourt & Wildside Press

MANUSCRIPT SUBMISSIONS:
Before sending us your manuscript, please send us a business-sized envelope, with postage affixed, addressed to you, for our guidelines. The address for this and all other editorial matters:
Weird Tales®, 123 Crooked Lane, King of Prussia PA 19406–2570
Visit our message board: http://www.wildsidepress.com
An e-mail version of our guidelines is also available for the asking from WEIRDTALES@COMCAST.NET
The address for subscriptions, subscribers' changes of address, advertising, and money matters is:
DNA Publications, Inc., PO Box 2988, Radford VA 24143–2988
Visit us on the Web at: DNAPUBLICATIONS.COM

Of course we read unsolicited submissions — but only by mail in standard manuscript format. To survive, all editors insist on a few Rules: each submission must be in proper format and must include a return envelope, addressed to you, with enough U.S. Postage affixed to bring the manuscript back to you. If you want us to discard the manuscript if we don't buy it, tell us so. In that case include a business-sized envelope, addressed to you, with U.S. Postage affixed, so we can send you our comments. No loose stamps, please.

We recommend two books on writing: *On Writing Science Fiction: the Editors Strike Back!* by Scithers, Schweitzer, & John M. Ford; $19.50, postpaid, in hardcovers from Owlswick Press, 123 Crooked Lane, King of Prussia PA 19406–2750. (We wrote it, so of course we speak highly of it.) In Pennsylvania, add $1.19 sales tax. The other is the always essential *The Elements of Style,* by William Strunk, Jr., & E.B. White, available from any good bookstore.

We are not responsible for manuscripts in our hands or in transit.
You must put your *name* and *address* on the first page of every manuscript. For all manuscripts:

`use 12-point type`

`on 24-point spacing, please!`

Certainly the look has changed since 1970. The hero *does* wear more clothes. His choice of weapons has broadened considerably. He usually has a stable of companions . . . a fellowship, you might say . . . often of various sexes, races, or species. It certainly seems that the influence of Tolkien overwhelmed that of Howard, even as the Frazetta-derived, iconic barbarian gave way to Aragorn wannabes, and to a host of amazons, and even George Alec Effinger's "Maureen Birnbaum, Barbarian Swordperson."

If you take away or change one element, is it still sword & sorcery? If the hero uses a bow, does that make it archery & sorcery? In this light, *did sword & sorcery ever exist in the first place,* or was it merely a subset of fantasy defined by its clichés? The closest analogy we can think of is the hardboiled detective story, which, like sword & sorcery, grew into a commercial category in the wake of a very small number of writers. (Arguably only two: Dashiell Hammett and Raymond Chandler.) Do mystery fans question if it's still hardboiled if the hero doesn't wear a trench coat, doesn't guzzle booze, drives a Volkswagon Beetle, and never slugs anybody? Or has mystery fiction outgrown the need for such definitions?

Regarding sword & sorcery, we think the jury is still out. Much of what was retrospectively lumped together into the "genre" had little in common before that point: Howard's Conan, Clark Ashton Smith's tales of Hyperborea and Zothique, Jack Vance's Dying Earth, Leiber's Fafhrd and the Gray Mouser, de Camp's Poseidonis and Jorian adventures, Moorcock's Elric, Charles Saunders's Imaro, and so on. Those stories have some elements in common, but their *mer-*

its, we suggest, have more to do with their differences. It is precisely because Leiber's or Moorcock's or de Camp's work constitutes an original vision, and is not a retread of Howard, that it is of interest.

Our recommendation to writers worrying about definitions: don't. Concentrate on a good story instead. Is Darrell Schweitzer's Sekenre series sword & sorcery? How about Keith Taylor's Kamose? They have all the elements, don't they? Sekenre even carried his father's old sword through part of the original novella, back in *Weird Tales*® #303. He has tended to use smaller cutlery since, or none at all. Sword & sorcery? Does Kamose ever use anything sharp while engaging in (or defending himself against) sorcery of the darkest hue? Does it actually matter?

To go back to the mystery-fiction analogy: everyone still loves Sherlock Holmes. The originals never go out of print. Countless Holmes pastiches are still being written and published. But wouldn't the detective story be in a sorry state if all detectives were still clones of Sherlock Holmes? Evolution is necessary.

What we're looking for in sword & sorcery fiction, if you want to call it that, are the virtues of the old masters: color, verve, drive, and — if you will — barbarian splendor, the exoticism of romance, the thrill (and chill) of midnight-dark meddlings in the supernatural. But we also want something with an original vision, something we haven't read before. Good fiction has to stand on its own, not merely remind us of something that we've already seen.

Sort of a movie review. Last issue we made an off-hand comment about Lovecraft movies,

"We've heard of a decent *Dagon* which went straight to video, but haven't seen it," with the implication that, maybe, just maybe, it was actually worth seeing.

Alas, no. **Dagon,** which seems to be co-produced by Brian Yuzna and The Fantastic Factory, directed by Stuart Gordon (he of *Re-animator* fame, so we had some hope for this) is, confusingly, an adaptation of Lovecraft's "The Shadow Over Innsmouth," starring a cast of unknowns and set on the Spanish coast. No objection to this last point, since the Deep Ones presumably roam the oceans and could just as readily set up a breeding colony in Spain as in Massachusetts. Whole sequences of the Lovecraft story are actually recognizable, which is more than can be said for some earlier adaptations (such as *Die, Monster, Die!* which is allegedly based on "The Colour Out of Space"). There are the inevitable changes. The hero is no longer a young, impoverished antiquarian on his *wanderjahr,* but a nerdy American millionaire with his (usually) scantily-clad girlfriend, accompanied by an older English couple (who are disposed of early on). Their boat is wrecked just off the Spanish town of Imboca, where things are very odd. The priest has webbed fingers. The guy at the desk in the run-down hotel has gills. There is only one "normal" person in the town, the cringing, yet garrulous town drunk Lovecraftians inevitably dub "Zadocko," whatever his actual name may have been.

Actually the development of the Zadock Allen character is one of *Dagon*'s few virtues. The town drunk, who alone has survived to tell of Imboca/Innsmouth's transformation into a den of squamous Dagon worshipers is seen in flashbacks as a sad-eyed boy, probably a pious

Catholic, who saw his parents killed and everything he ever believed in torn away from him. He survived because he took to the bottle and was seen as harmless or even mad. In the film, in what is otherwise a gratuitously gory scene, "Zadocko" gains some dignity and redemption at his death.

Other than that, there is little good we can say about *Dagon*. It is very muddled and, at times, gratuitously and pointlessly gory. The Imbocans kill all strangers who arrive in their town. Men are skinned alive. (Why? Do the Deep Ones actually care?) Women are either killed or left to be raped (and then killed?) by the "god" of the town, a vast, tentacular monstrosity, which might be the entity of the title, for all it doesn't much resemble what Lovecraft described. (Remember, there actually was a Lovecraft story called "Dagon." This movie is not based on it.) While such atrocities are going on, the crazed, shambling townspeople (they *do* shamble in fine form, we admit) chant "Iä! Cthulhu fhtagn!" which causes considerable confusion as to which entity is being invoked.

But more seriously, this film lacks the right *sensibility*. It's coarse, vulgar, and dumb, like Stuart Gordon's other films, only lacking the sense of parody which made *Re-Animator* work. And, *Re-Animator,* of course, was based on six of the very *worst* Lovecraft stories, and fully worthy of them. It was good, campy fun.

We'd always suspected, though, that the people who made that sort of movie would not be able to do justice to major, *good* Lovecraft, and now, alas, that suspicion has been confirmed.

A correction: In our 80th anni-versary issue, #331, the resplendent artwork for Charles L. Harness's "The Melkart Coin" is mistakenly accredited to Russell Morgan. Not that we don't think Russell Morgan's art isn't resplendent also, but these drawings (as doubtless our experienced readers must have suspected) were actually the work of **George Barr.**

Congratulations are in order to our cover artist **Jason Van Hollander,** for winning the International Horror Guild Award for Best Artist of 2002, and to our interior artist, **Allen Koszowski** for being made Artist Guest of Honor at the World Fantasy Convention, to be held in Washington, D.C. this coming Halloween. (We hope to see many of you there!)

The Most Popular Story in issue 331, as well as 332, will have to wait (again) because our schedule seems to be so staggered that we're putting this issue out before we've had much response. Our correspondents have also been remiss, alas. We did, however, receive the following challenging epistle from **Wilum Pugmire:**

Found your 80th Anniversary issue yesterday, with its superb cover. Strangely, although it is not black, the red-robed figure reminded me of Nyarlathotep, ushering in the death of mortality. It's quite a striking image, your finest cover since Summer 2002. Many hearty congratulations on your 80th anniversary. It brought back memories of WT 50, with essays on writing for Weird Tales® by those WT authors who still lived. I was a young Lovecraftian at the time, driving to Tacoma every week so as to visit H. Warner Munn. Harold would read to me the stories he wrote for WT, and would tell of driving HPL to various New England sites.

Thinking of this made me dig out my Xerox® copies of Munn's letters from WT, which Munn let me duplicate. On the reverse of one letter is the only time Wright spelled out his complete last name, in light pencil that barely shows on the Xerox® copy. I have no idea if the Munn family kept these letters after Harold's death. I still remember the look of woe upon his face when Harold told me of burning many papers when he made the move from New England to Washington State; among these destroyed letters were all of his correspondence from Lovecraft.

I've seen very few old issues of WT, but I've read much of its fiction in Arkham House books, paperback reprints, etc. etc. Except for the occasional cover, the new WT doesn't feel like the "Golden Age" of WT. Part of this, I think, is that you publish much that seems straight fantasy. Perhaps this is why Ellen Datlow in the April Locus expressed her opinion that you don't actually publish horror. I am not certain that I understand what she means by that; but I agree that you almost never publish any fiction that feels like "classic" horror, as we've come to understand it from what we consider to be the classic horror fiction from Weird Tales®'s past. Such a thing would perhaps be impossible; the world has altered too utterly, and so has our vision.

The huge change in WT is that you publish, now, extremely good, well-written fiction, with very few losers. The only stinker I remember in recent years was the awful "Graveyard" by Michael Mayhew, in 324. Not only was I dismayed that you could publish such a bad story, but I was astounded that you didn't change its pathetic title!

In this Spring 2003 issue, you published some very good horror fiction. And you have a story by

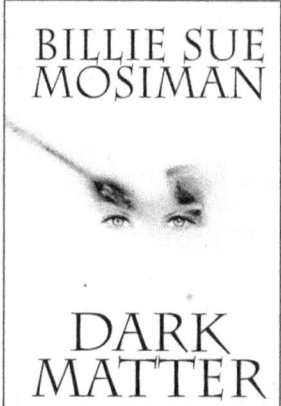

one who will be regarded as a "classic" fifty years hence, the amazing Thomas Ligotti.

I confess that "Blood Chess" feels more like fantasy than horror. Although Tanith Lee writes beautifully, I simply don't find her fiction interesting; it fails to captivate.

The delightful surprise of the issue was Keith Taylor's superb "The Company of the Gods," which had a taste of Bob Bloch's tales of haunted Ægypt, of "Luveh-Keraph, priest of cryptic Bast," penned many decades gone for Weird Tales *and* Strange Stories. *Taylor gets it exactly right and his story is one that I'll return to.*

I look forward to many more issues of Weird Tales. *And if I'm doom'd to live another twenty years, at least I know that I can help you celebrate your first 100 years!*

Yes, we *do* entertain ambitions of editing the 100th anniversary of *Weird Tales*®. It's physically possible, without resorting to essential "saltes" and eldritch sorcery. Why, none of us are anywhere near a hundred years old. Yet. . . .

As for the Ellen Datlow remark in *Locus*, we admit that it puzzled us too, particularly when she then went on to reprint Stephen Gallagher's exemplary horror story, "Little Dead Girl Singing," from *WT 327*, in her *Year's Best Fantasy and Horror*. We don't publish horror? No *classic* horror? We need only point to Brian Lumley's "Fruiting Bodies," Alan Rodgers's "Emma's Daughter," Chet Williamson's "Jabbie Welsh," Stephen King's "The Glass Floor," or *any* of the Thomas Ligotti stories we've run over the years. It is silly to say we *do not* publish horror. We wouldn't argue with anyone who says that we don't publish horror *exclusively*, and an exclusive, 100-percent straight diet of horror, horror, and nothing but horror is what some people seem to want.

But that was *never* what *Weird Tales*® was about, even in the 1930s. Our policy has always been to run *Weird Tales*® as if the original magazine had continued to the present day, not as a fossil or re-creation of something 50 years gone, but as a *living magazine* which continues to evolve.

After all, we we are the direct descendant of the magazine which had room for Conan the Barbarian, Clark Ashton Smith's sublime "Xeethra" or "Sadastor," C.L. Moore's tales of Northwest Smith and Jirel of Joiry, and even Jack Williamson's lost-city adventure, *Golden Blood*. Not exclusively horror. Horror mixed in with other forms, in non- contemporary settings. If Clark Ashton Smith could set horror stories in ancient Hyperborea or on the planet Mars, we don't see why "horror" needs to be defined as narrowly as some people define it today. Call it fantasy-horror, then.

See you next issue. We want your letters! Snail mail to 123 Crooked Lane, King of Prussia PA 19406–2570, e-mail to Weirdtales@comcast.net .   Ω

SHADOWINGS

by Douglas E. Winter

"Hark — hark — hark! He comes on the wings of the storm. Oh, it is most horrible — horrible!"
— *Varney the Vampire, or the Feast of Blood* (1845–47)

Not another vampire novel.

These days the very sight of the V-word on a book jacket prompts a shiver of dread — not of creaking coffins and the risen dead, but of a repetitive reading disorder.

Introduced to Anglo-American literature by John Polidori's skewering of Lord Byron in "The Vampyre" (1819) and made popular by the "penny dreadful" *Varney the Vampire* (1845–47) and, of course, Bram Stoker's *Dracula* (1897), stories of bloodthirsty immortals have beguiled readers for centuries; but when Stephen King and Anne Rice opened the jugular of commerce with *'Salem's Lot* (1975) and *Interview with the Vampire* (1976), the culture industry gorged. Vampires became merchandise, packaged into sagas and series, hunted by demographically correct divas named Buffy and Anita Blake, wrought by a legion of lesser hands into cliché and caricature.

At first glance, then, it's surprising to find Elizabeth Knox, a gifted New Zealander whose complex prose has summoned comparisons to Jane Austen and Charlotte Brontë, apparently slumming among the gravestones. Yet Knox, who danced with angels in *The Vintner's Luck* (1998) and fractured time in the daunting *Black Oxen* (2000), plainly loves a challenge; and *Daylight* (Ballantine, hardcover, 356 pp., $23.95) confronts a worthy one: the redemption of a tarnished icon.

Brian "Bad" Phelan, an Auckland policeman wounded by a terrorist bomb, seeks escape along the French-Italian border but encounters "a series of spurious connections — indecent, unreasonable connections." The corpse of a woman floats in the Mediterranean off Riomaggiore, tossed on the waves at the mouth of a sea cave. Her strangely mottled hair matches that of a woman he'd seen die in a caving accident a decade earlier — a woman whose face was mirrored in a painting he glimpsed at the moment of the terror explosion. Phelan volunteers to retrieve the corpse, hoping that the act will cleanse him of the experience, which "had filled his soul with gloom, a shrapnel of small shadows"; but the shadows, and his wounds, only deepen.

The dead woman is Martine Dardo — namesake of the Blessed Martine Raimondi of Dardo, a martyred nun to whom she bore an uncanny resemblance. Like Countess Mircalla Karnstein and the eponym of the first great vampire story, J. Sheridan LeFanu's "Carmilla" (1872), the women are one and the same, of course; but nothing is so simple in the wonder-worlds of Elizabeth Knox. Phelan is witness to a startling trinity: Martine; her friend Eve Moskelute; and Eve's twin, Dawn, whose parti-colored hair marks her as another émigré to eternal darkness.

Phelan's investigation of Martine's second death turns into a crimson seduction as it entwines with the inquiries of Father Daniel Octave, the Jesuit postulator for Martine's ascent to sainthood (even if it means blinking back unruly facts) and the machinations of the novel's Ugly American, Tom Hilxen, for whom vampirism is a natural extension of consumerism.

These lives crash and churn like the waves beneath Riomaggiore as the plot leaps continents and decades, spiraling back to 18th-century dilettante Guy de Chambord, whose lurid novel "Lumiere du Jour" — yes, "Daylight" — reveals the origin of an enigmatic King Vampire, Ila.

The mystery of the Venerable Martine and her *tedium vitae* will inevitably test Octave's faith and bring Ila into the light; while for Phelan, those "spurious connections" question his surrender to happenstance.

In celebrating Wilkie Collins's *The Woman in White* (1860), which brought horror home from the distant castles and abbeys of Old Europe, Henry James challenged the relevance of the Gothic Romance made famous by Mrs. Radcliffe and transfigured by Jane Austen in *Northanger Abbey* (1818).

CLASSIC PULP FICTION FROM WILDSIDE PRESS!

Satan's Daughter and Other Tales from the Pulps

by E. Hoffmann Price. Intro by Darrell Schweitzer

A baker's dozen of classic pulp stories, by a master of the genre! *Satan's Daughter and Other Tales from the Pulps* includes such rare gems as the title story, "Scourge of the Silver Dragon," "Revolt of the Damned," "Pit of Madness," "The Walking Dead," "Drink or Draw," and many more. A delightful selection, ranging from fantasy to horror to action-mystery, all sprinkled with a dash of erotica.

Out of the Wreck and Other Nautical Tales

by Captain A. E. Dingle

Captain A.E. Dingle published sea stories in the pulp magazines for decades, and the volume, quality and variety of his tales is nothing short of astonishing. This collection assembles eight of his finest, from the Sherlock Holmes pastiche "Watson!" to the short novel "The Coolie Ship," from the misadventures of "Skimps, Ship's Boy" to the lives of "Hard-Shell Clammers" -- nautical stories told by a master craftsman!

The Mysterious Wu Fang: Case of the Suicide Tomb

by Robert J. Hogan

The ancient tomb had been sealed for a thousand years; its discovery was an archaeological find. But few guessed its horrible secret, or knew that an Oriental super-villain, the fiendish Wu Fang, wished to enter its portals to capture the death germs buried there -- deadly germs of a rare plague of madness which he meant to use to control the world! From the December, 1935 issue of *The Mysterious Wu Fang* magazine, presented with its original cover and interior art.

Operator #5: Blood Reign of the Dictator

by Curtis Steele

Operator #5 appeared in more than 48 novels in the pulp magazine bearing his name. From April 1934 to November 1939, Jimmy Christopher fought villains from inside the United States and invaders from without. With World War II looming on the horizon, the Operator #5 books became a reflection of the times -- none more so than when a fascist dictator appears to take over the U.S. government! *Blood Reign of the Dictator* is a classic entry in the series.

Secret Agent "X": The Legions of the Living Dead

by Brant House

From the September, 1935 issue of *Secret Agent X* comes this sensational novel: "From nowhere hurtled that black death car. And from nowhere came its grisly occupants. They were not of the earth, for their human flesh was immune to bullets. They were not of the grave, for they manned the wheel and a blasting machine gun- Secret Agent "X" made a desperate maneuver to block their invasion of the land of the living. And in that weird terror trap, he came face to face with a man he knew had died five years ago!"

"What are the Appenines to us," James asked, "or we to the Appenines?"

Daylight is Knox's riposte, urging that the Appenines, like Transylvania, exist beyond geography in a realm of the imagination, a vital dreamscape where the past survives, stripped of the dubious veneer of "civilization." Their fanged inhabitants — whether named Dracula or Lestat or Ila — unleash the secret history that has been bleached of grime and tears and blood by the bright light of "progress," and offer guilt-free fantasies of intellect and flesh. Cerebral, cultured, and noble (if not aristocratic), these avatars of impossible romance and immortality are nonetheless feral in their passions, whether sensual or for blood. But fantasies, Knox urges, are mirrors of reality, and do not exist without consequences. Doomed to night and shadow, her vampires offer the ominous prospect that "progress" is the true monster — and remind us that daylight and illumination are very different things.

In *Daylight,* Elizabeth Knox has written a *Northanger Abbey* for the new century — an entertaining fiction that offers a potent summation and critique of a weary genre. Her style is meticulous and dreamlike, moving with a languor worthy of its nightwalkers. She demands and deserves a careful reading, because there is no doubt:

Daylight is not another vampire novel.

As the vampire winged its way toward commercial success in the 1980s, its potential for mystery and metaphor — and good, old-fashioned blood-letting — was supplanted by a formidable foe: the zombie. Given terrifying new life in the now- legendary "living dead" films of George A. Romero and taken to a gory apotheosis by director Lucio Fulci in the likes of *Zombi 2* ("Zombie"/ "Zombie Flesheaters") (1979), *Paura nella città dei morti viventi* ("City of the Living Dead/ "The Gates of Hell") (1980), and *E tu vivrai nel terrore . . . L'Aldilà* ("The Beyond") (1981), the zombie lurched into the pages of late twentieth- century horror fiction without regard for vodoun tradition, transformed into a monster of mindlessness whose sole ambition was to add to its ranks through cannibalism.There was no better icon for a society bent on buying its way into comfort, conformity, and sociopolitical correctness.

Only a handful of satisfying zombie novels have been written over the past two decades — King's *Pet Sematary* (1983) and Thomas Tessier's *Finishing Touches* (1985) among them — leaving many of the zombie's memorable incarnations to come courtesy of the *Books of the Dead,* edited by John Skipp and Craig Spector. Intended as an homage to Romero's

films — which, in turn, had their genesis in Richard Matheson's *I Am Legend* (1954) and B-movies like *Invisible Invaders* (1959) — *Book of the Dead* (1989), *Still Dead: Book of the Dead II* (1992), and the unpublished *Book of the Dead III* were vital manifestos that embraced, sometimes to the point of suffocation, the ideal of a horror without limits. Their stories raged, sometimes merely for the sake of rage, but more often against the Reaganite dream of a nation spent into passivity — and against the increasingly calculated and safe genre that sought to pass for horror fiction.

By the time *Still Dead* saw print, its "splatterpunk" sizzle had been co-opted, chit-chatted, and (most important) written into irrelevance. Bret Easton Ellis brought its confrontational impulses into the mainstream with *American Psycho* (1991), and the splatpack's original question — how far could you go? — had been replaced by the inevitable one: how low could you go?

The descent of the living dead into the generic was heralded by the first wave of recycling — Fulci's *Zombi 3* (1988) and the remake of *Night of the Living Dead* (1990) — but the reintegration of the zombie into the realm of genre has been perfected in the *Books of the Flesh* trilogy of original fiction edited by James Lowder. *The Book of All Flesh, The Book of More Flesh,* and now *The Book of Final Flesh* (Eden Studios, trade paperback, 320 pp., $16.95) obviously emulate the *Books of the Dead,* which signals a salient problem: Paying homage to an homage is something like releasing a tribute album to a cover band.

Complicating matters is the fact that the *Books of the Flesh* are companions to a "zombie survival horror" rôle-playing game, the appetizingly titled *All Flesh Must Be Eaten.* Lowder is expansive in his tastes, however, and the stories are not limited to a shared world or even a shared vision, but range from Romero-like apocalypses to voodoo and even science-fiction scenarios. Not surprisingly, the name recognition factor is low; and although the stories have craft, there's a decided lack of heart . . . and guts.

Gone are the transgressive impulses that powered the Romero/Fulci films and the *Books of the Dead* (although Tim Waggoner works some mojo in "Provider"). Instead we have stories that seem written less from inspiration than from participation: If you build an anthology, they will come — and, apparently, keep coming. Scratch the word "zombie" in favor of, say, "Yeti," and not many of these stories would require much in the way of revision.

Within a few paragraphs, most texts leap into unreality — not a parallel world capable of invasion

by the fantastic or the supernatural, but one of make-believe, those impossible places that exist only in stories (and that don't require messy things like the suspension of disbelief, characterization, metaphor, meaning). Too many writers are interested in "concept" — or, to be harsh but honest, gimmick — than in emotion. In "Homelands," for example, an obviously talented Lucien Soulban contemplates invisible zombies in a post-apocalyptic Shanghai — but why? Only one such story, Paul G. Tremblay's "So Many Things Left Out," which posits an undead Samuel Clemens, really answers that question.

Emotion — and an understanding that a zombie is something more than a monster — are what makes two other stories stand out: Scott Edelman's "The Last Supper," a sly fable that inverts *I Am Legend,* and Barry Hollander's "Familiar Eyes." Otherwise, there's little flesh here, and far too many dry bones.

Lullaby (Doubleday, hardcover, 261 pp., $24.95) is the fifth novel by Chuck Palahuink, and his first to evoke explicitly supernatural themes, underscoring the bittersweet fact that non-genre horror is thriving. Anguished newspaper reporter Carl Streator tumbles to the story of his life while covering Sudden Infant Death Syndrome: The same book, a collection of children's poetry, is present at the scene of each death he chronicles — and one of its entries, derived from an African "culling song," proves lethal when recited. Written with scathing wit and bursts of adrenaline and testosterone (Palahuink is, after all, the author of *Fight Club*), *Lullaby* goes off-key when Streator and a surreal scrum of sidekicks set off on Palahuink's by-now inevitable road trip; but this is great, unstoppable fiction from a great and hopefully unstoppable writer.

A similar plot frames *The Buzzing* (Vintage, trade paperback, 272 pp., $12.00), a likable but ultimately disappointing first novel by Jim Knipfel (better known for the memoirs *Slackjaw* and *Quitting the Nairobi Trio*). Another fading reporter, Roscoe Baragon — surnamed for the big burrowing beastie of Toho Studios' *Frankenstein Conquers the World* (1965) and *Destroy All Monsters* (1968) — discerns a puzzling pattern in a series of apparently arbitrary encounters, and begins to question reality . . . or his own sanity. But the too-familiar premise and the torn-from-the-tabloids (and Toho films) conspiracies-within-conspiracies constrain both the comedy and the terror, leaving Baragon in a well-told web of paranoia about nothing that particularly matters to the reader.

A news reporter is merely one disguise assumed by "MM" — the maniacal multiple personalities who narrate this season's most unlikely thriller, *Bunker 13* by Aniruddha Bahal (Farrar, Straus & Giroux, hardcover, 345 pp., $24.00). Imagine Bret Easton Ellis reincarnated in India with a trailer full of meth and M-203 grenade launchers, let loose to meditate upon the unending Indo-Pakistani conflict and its attendant corruption, greed, malice, and bigotry. Forget the fact that this novel — written entirely in second person and in an English-as-a-second-language voice, with a plot that makes James Bond movies seem plausible — would be considered unpublishable if submitted by an American. Grin and grimace instead, and enjoy the bumpy ride to its eye-widening finale.

In *Repetition* (Grove Press, hardcover, 178 pp., $23.00), Alain Robbe-Grillet, the master of narrative fragmentation and recurring imagery, returns with his first novel (save for his "autobiography") in twenty years, which trumps recent motion pictures inspired by his work, including *Memento* (2001) and *Irreversible* (2002). The putative narrator, Henri Robin, is an agent of the French Secret Service who, upon entering post-World War Two Berlin, is promptly confronted by a vision of a doppelgänger. As Robin pursues his unspoken but deadly mission, a second narrator interrupts to note inconsistencies and annotate the text with contradictory and increasingly obsessive footnotes; and Robin, like the novel itself, begins to fragment into a mosaic of fading memories and erotica that may or may not offer truth. This is a rare, if difficult, novel that, although occasionally too clever for its own good, delights the patient reader with its daring and its singularity. The uninitiated will no doubt find an easier introduction to Robbe-Grillet in his first published novel, *Les Gommes* ("The Erasers") (1953).

In contemporary horror, Robbe-Grillet's devious mazes are matched only by the dreamscapes of Thomas Ligotti, whose *Sideshow and Other Stories* (Subterranean Press, limited-edition chapbook, 32 pp., hardcover, $75.00, softcover, $12.00, sold out on publication), offers an exquisitely elusive set of vignettes said to have been written by an anonymous gentleman whom the narrator befriended in a late-night coffee shop. This brief collection considers the "essentially show business nature" of life — which, its mysterious writer-within-a-writer urges, is "no more than sideshow business." The stories — in fact, achingly atmospheric prose poems — ponder subterfuge, damnation, and — inevitably — the trope of the double. *Sideshow* deserves an immediate reprint.   Ω

THE TOWN MANAGER

by Thomas Ligotti

illustrated by Jason Van Hollander

One gray morning some weeks before the onset of winter, some troubling news had swiftly travelled among us: the town manager was not in his office and seemed nowhere to be found. We allowed this situation, or apparent situation, to remain tentative for as long as we could. This was simply how we had handled such developments in the past.

It was Carnes, the man who operated the trolley which ran up and down Main Street, who initially recognized the possibly that the town manager was no longer with us. He was the first one who noticed, as he was walking from his house located at one end of town to the trolley station at the other end, that the dim lamp which had always remained switched on inside the town manager's office was now off.

Of course, it was not beyond all credibility that the light bulb in the lamp that stood in the corner of the town manager's desk had simply burned out or that there had been a short circuit in the electrical system of the small office along Main Street. There might even have been a more extensive power failure that also affected the rooms above the office, where the town manager had resided since he had first arrived among us to assume his duties. Certainly we all knew the town manager as someone who was in no way vigilant regarding the state of either his public office or his private living quarters. Consequently, those of us in the crowd that had gathered outside the town manager's office, and his home, considered both the theory of an expired light bulb and that of an electrical short circuit at some length. Yet all the while, our agitation only increased. Carnes was the one whose anxiety over this matter was the most severe, for the present state of affairs had afflicted him longer than anyone else, if only by a few minutes. As I have already indicated, this was not the first time that we had been faced with such a development. So when Carnes finally called for action, the rest of us soon abandoned our refuge in the theoretical. "It's time to do something," said the trolley driver. "We have to know."

Ritter, who ran the local hardware store, jimmied open the door to the town manager's office, and several of us were soon searching around inside. The place was fairly neat, if only by virtue of being prac-

tically unfurnished. There was simply a chair, a desk, and the lamp on top of the desk. The rest of it was just empty floor space and bare walls. Even the drawers of the desk, as some of the more curious members of our search party discovered, were all empty. Ritter was checking the wall socket into which the lamp's cord was plugged, and someone else was inspecting the fuse box at the back of the office. But these were merely stall tactics. No one wanted to reach under the lamp shade and click the switch to find out whether the bulb had merely burned out or, more ominously, if that place had been given over to darkness by design. The latter action, as all of us were aware, signaled that the tenure of any given town manager was no longer in effect.

At one time, there had been a great chandelier which hung in the town hall located at the south end of Main Street. When that structure fell into decay and finally had to be abandoned, other buildings gave out their illumination, from the upper floors of the old opera house (also vacated in the course of time) to the present storefront office that more recently had served as the center of the town's civic administration. But there always came a day when, without notice to anyone in the town, the light went out.

"He's not upstairs," Carnes yelled down to us from the town manager's private rooms. At that precise moment, I had taken it upon myself to try the light switch. The bulb lit up, and everyone in the room went mute. After a time, somebody-to this day I cannot recall who it was-stated in a resigned voice, "He has left us."

Those were the words that passed through the crowd outside the town manager's office . . . until everyone knew the truth. No one even speculated that this development might have been caused by mischief or a mistake. The only conclusion was that the old town manager was no longer in control and that a new appointment would be made, if in fact this had not already been done.

Nonetheless, we still had to go through the motions. Throughout the rest of that gray morning and into the afternoon, a search was conducted.

© 2003 Jason Van Hollander

Over the course of my life, these searches were performed with increasingly greater speed and efficiency whenever one town manager turned up missing as the prelude to the installation of another. The buildings and houses comprising our town were now far fewer than in my childhood and youth. Whole sections that had once been districts of prolific activity had been transformed by a remarkable corrosion into empty lots where only a few bricks and some broken glass indicated that anything besides weeds and desiccated earth had ever existed there. During my years of youthful ambition, I had determined that one day I would have a house in a grand neighborhood known as The Hill. This area was still known as such, a designation bitterly retained even though the real estate in question — now a rough and empty stretch of ground — no longer rose to a higher elevation than the land surrounding it.

After satisfying ourselves that the town manager was nowhere to be found within the town, we moved out into the countryside. Just as we were going through the motions when we searched inside the town limits, we continued going through the motions as we tramped through the landscape beyond them. The time of year was so close to the onset of winter, and there were only a few bare trees to obstruct our view in any direction as we wandered over the hardening earth. We kept our eyes open, but we could not pretend to be meticulous searchers.

In the past, no town manager had ever been found, either alive or dead, once he had gone missing and the light in his office had been turned off. Our only concern was to act in such a way that would allow us to report to the new town manager, when he appeared, that we had made an effort to discover the whereabouts of his predecessor. Yet this ritual seemed to matter less and less to each successive town manager, the most recent of whom barely acknowledged our attempts to uncover the dead or living body of the previous administrator. "What?" he said as he sat dozing behind the desk in his office.

"We did the best we could," repeated one of us who had led the search, which on that occasion had taken place in early spring. "It stormed the entire time," said another.

After hearing our report, the town manager merely replied, "Oh, I see. Yes, well done." Then he dismissed us and returned to his nap.

"Why do we even bother?" said Leeman the barber when were outside the town manager's office. "We never find anything."

I referred him and the others to the section of the town charter, a brief document to be sure, that required "a fair search of the town and its environs"

whenever a town manager went missing. This was part of an arrangement that had been made by the founders and that had been upheld throughout succeeding generations. Unfortunately, nothing in the records that had come to be stored in the new opera house, and were subsequently lost to the same fire that destroyed this shoddily constructed building some years before, had ever overtly stated with whom this arrangement had been made. (The town charter itself was now only a few poorly phrased notes assembled from recollections and lore, although the specifics of this rudimentary document were seldom disputed.) At the time, no doubt, the founders had taken what seemed the best course for the survival and prosperity of the town, and they forged an arrangement that committed their descendants to this same course. There was nothing extraordinary about such actions and agreements.

"But that was years ago," said Leeman on that rainy spring afternoon. "I for one think that it's time to find out just who we're dealing with."

Others agreed with him. I myself did not disagree. Nonetheless, we never did manage to broach the subject with the old town manager. But as we walked across the countryside on that day so close to the onset of winter, we talked among ourselves and vowed that we would pose certain questions to the new town manager, who usually arrived not long after the disappearance or abdication of the previous administrator, sometimes on the very same day.

The first matter we wished to take up was the reason we were required to conduct a futile search for missing town managers. Some of us believed that these searches were merely a way of distracting us, so that the new town manager could take office before anyone had a chance to observe by what means he had arrived or from what direction he came. Others were of the opinion that these expeditions did in fact serve some purpose, although what that may have been was beyond our understanding. Either way, we were all agreed that it was time for the town — that is, what there was left of it — to enter a new and more enlightened era in its history. However, by the time we reached the ruined farmhouse, all our resolutions dissolved into the grayness in which that day had been enveloped.

Traditionally, the ruined farmhouse, along with the wooden shed that stood nearby it, marked the point at which we ended our search and returned to town. It was now close to sundown, which would give us just enough time to be back in our homes before dark once we had made a perfunctory inspection of the farmhouse and its shed. But we never made it that far. This time we kept our distance from that farmhouse, which was no more than a jagged and tilting outline against the gray sky, as well as from the shed, a narrow structure of thin wooden planks that someone had hammered together long ago. There was something written across those weathered boards, markings that none of us had ever seen before. They were scored into the wood, as if with a sharp blade. Some of the letters were either missing or unreadable in the places where they were gouged into planks that had separated from one another. Carnes the trolley man was standing at my side.

"Does that say what I think it says," he said to me, almost in a whisper.

"I think so."

"And the light inside?"

"Like smoldering embers," I said concerning the reddish glow that was shining through the wooden slats of the shed.

Having recognized the arrival of the new town manager — from whatever direction and by whatever means he may have come — we all turned away and walked silently toward town, pacing slowly through the gray countryside that day by day was being seized by the coming winter.

Despite what we had come across during our search of the countryside that day, we soon reconciled ourselves to it, or at least had reached a point where we no longer openly expressed our anxiety. Did it really matter if, rather than occupying a building on Main Street with a sign that read "Town Manager" over the door, the one who now held this position chose to occupy a shed whose rotting wooden planks had roughly the same words inscribed upon them with a sharp blade? Things always had been moving in that direction. At one time the town manager conducted business from a suite of offices located in the town hall and lived in a fine house in The Hill district of town. Now this official would be working out of a weather-beaten shed next to a ruined farmhouse. Nothing remained the same for very long. Change was the very essence of our lives.

My own situation was typical. As previously mentioned, I had ambitions of owning a residence in The Hill district. For a time I operated a delivery business that almost certainly would have led to my attaining this goal. However, by the time the old town manager arrived, I was sweeping the floors at Leeman's barbershop and taking whatever odd jobs came along. In any case, my drive to build up a successful delivery business was all but extinguished once The Hill district had eroded away to nothing.

Perhaps the general decline in the conditions of the town, as well as the circumstances of its residents, could be attributed to poor officiating on the part of our town managers, who in many ways seemed to be less and less able in their duties as one succeeded the other over the years. Whatever apprehensions we had about the new town manager, it could not be said that the old town manager was a model administer. For some time before his term came to an end, he spent the whole of each working day asleep behind his desk.

On the other hand, every town manager could be credited with introducing some element of change, some official project of one kind or another, that was difficult to condemn as wholly detrimental. Even if the new opera house had never been anything but a shoddily constructed firetrap, it nonetheless represented an effort at civic rehabilitation, or seemed to be such. For his part, the old manager was responsible for the trolley which ran up and down Main Street. In the early days of his administration, he brought in workers from outside the town to construct this monument to his spirit of innovation. Not that there had ever been a great outcry for such a conveyance in our town, which could easily be traversed from one end to the other either on foot or by bicycle without causing the least exertion to those of us who were in reasonably good health. Nevertheless, once the trolley had been built, most of us did make use of it at one time or another, if only for the novelty of it. Some people, for whatever reason, made regular use of this new means of transportation and even seemed to depend on it to carry them the distance of only a few blocks. If nothing else, the trolley provided Carnes with regular employment, which he had not formerly enjoyed.

In brief, we had always managed to adapt to the ways of each town manager who had been sent to us. The difficult part was waiting for new administrators to reveal the nature of their plans for the town and then adjusting ourselves to whatever form they might take. This was the system in which we had functioned for generations. This was the order of things into which we had been born and to which we had committed ourselves by compliance. The risk of opposing this order, of plunging into the unknown,

was simply too much for us to contemplate for very long. But we did not foresee, despite having witnessed the spectacle of the shed beside the ruined farmhouse, that the town was about to enter a radically new epoch in its history.

The first directive from the new town manager was communicated to us by a torn piece of paper that came skipping down the sidewalk of Main Street one day and was picked up by an old woman, who showed it to the rest of us. The paper was made from a pulpy stock and was brownish in color. The writing on the paper looked as if it had been made with charred wood and resembled the same hand that had written those words across the old boards of the town manager's shed. The message was this: **DUSTROY TROLY.**

While the literal sense of these words was apparent enough, we were reluctant to act upon a demand that was so obscure in its point and purpose. It was not unprecedented for a new town manager to obliterate some structure or symbol that marked the administration of the one who had come before him, so that the way might be cleared for him to erect a defining structure or symbol of his own, or simply to efface any prominent sign of the previous order and thereby display the presence of a new one. But usually some reason was offered, some excuse was made, for taking this action. This obviously was not the case with the town manager's instruction to destroy the trolley. So we decided to do nothing until we received some enhancement regarding this matter. Ritter suggested that we might consider composing a note of our own to request further instructions. This note could be left outside the door of the town manager's shed. Not surprisingly, there were no volunteers for this mission. And until we received a more detailed notice, the trolley would remain intact.

The following morning the trolley came tooting down Main Street for its first run of the day. However, it made no stops for those waiting along the sidewalk. "Look at this," Leeman said to me as he stared out the front window of his barbershop. Then he went outside. I set my broom against a wall and joined him. Others were already standing on the street, watching the trolley until it finally came to rest at the other end of town. "There was no one at the switch," said Leeman, an observation that a number of persons echoed. When it seemed that the trolley was not going to make a return trip, several of us walked down the street to investigate. When we entered the vehicle, we found the naked body of Carnes the trolley driver lying on the floor. He had been severely mutilated and was dead. Burned into his chest were the words: **DUSTROY TROLY.**

We spent the next few days doing exactly that. We also pulled up the tracks that ran the length of the town and tore down the electrical system that had powered the trolley. Just as we were completing these labors, someone spotted another piece of that torn, brownish paper. It was being pushed about by the wind in the sky above us, jerking about like a kite. Eventually it descended into our midst. Standing in a circle around the piece of paper, we read the scrawled words of the message. GUD, it said. NXT YUR JBS WULL CHNG.

Not only did our jobs change, but so did the entire face of the town. Once again, workmen came from outside with orders to perform various kinds of construction, demolition, and decoration that began along Main Street and ultimately extended into the outlying neighborhoods. We had been instructed by the usual means not to interfere with them. Throughout the deep gray winter, they worked on the interiors of the town's buildings. With the coming of spring, they finished off the exteriors and were gone. What they left behind them was a place that did not resemble a town as much as it did a carnival funhouse. And those of us who lived there functioned as sideshow freaks once we had been notified, by the usual method, of exactly how our jobs had changed.

For example, Ritter's Hardware had been emptied of its traditional merchandise and restructured as an elaborate maze of lavatories. Upon entering the front door you immediately found yourself standing between a toilet and a sink. Built into one of the walls of this small room was another door that opened upon another lavatory that was somewhat larger in dimensions. This room had two doors that led to further lavatories, some of which could be located only by ascending a spiral staircase or walking down a long, narrow corridor. Each lavatory differed somewhat in size and d,cor. None of the lavatories was functional. The exterior of Ritter's Hardware was a given a new façade constructed of large stone blocks and a pair of fake towers standing on either side of the building and rising some distance above it. A sign above the front door designated the former hardware store as "Comfort Castle." Ritter's new job was to sit in a chair on the sidewalk outside his former place of business wearing a simple uniform with the word "Attendant" displayed in sewn lettering below the left shoulder.

Leeman the barber was even less fortunate in the new career that had been assigned to him. His shop, renamed "Baby Town," had been refurbished into a gigantic playpen. Amid stuffed animals and an array of toys, Leeman was required to languish in infants' clothing sized for an adult.

All of the businesses along Main Street had been

transformed in some manner, although their tone was not always as whimsical as Ritter's Comfort Castle or Leeman's Baby Town. A number of the buildings appeared simply as abandoned storefronts . . . until one explored the interior and discovered that the back room was actually a miniature movie theater where foreign cartoons were projected upon a bare wall or that located in the basement was an art gallery filled entirely with paintings and sketches of questionable taste. Sometimes these abandoned storefronts were precisely what they appeared to be, except you would find yourself locked inside once the door had closed, forcing you to exit out the back.

Behind the stores of Main Street was a world of alleys where it was perpetually night, an effect created by tunnel-like arcades enclosing this vast area. Dim lamps were strategically placed so that no stretch of alley was entirely in darkness as you wandered between high wooden fences or brick walls. Many of the alleys ended up in someone's kitchen or living room, allowing an escape back into the town. Some of them kept growing more and more narrow until no further progress was possible and every step leading to this point needed to be retraced. Other alleys gradually altered in their backdrops, and eventually the scene changed from that of a small town to one of a big city where screams and sirens could be heard in the distance, although they were only recordings piped in through hidden speakers. It was in these precincts, where painted theatrical backdrops of tall tenement buildings with zig-zagging fire escapes rose up on every side, that I worked at my own new job.

At the terminus of an obscure alley where steam was pumped through the holes of a false sewer grating, I had been stationed in a kiosk where I sold soup in paper cups. To be more accurate, it was not actually soup that I was given to sell but something more like bullion. Behind the counter that fronted my kiosk there was a thin mattress on the floor where I could sleep at night, or whenever I felt like sleeping, since it seemed unlikely that any customers would venture through that labyrinth of alleys so that I might serve them. I subsisted on my own bullion and the water I used to concoct this desolate repast. It seemed to me that the new town manager would finally succeed in the task which his predecessors had but lazily pursued over the years: that of bleeding the town of the few resources that had been left to it. I could not have been more wrong in this assessment.

Within a matter of weeks, I had a steady stream of customers lined up outside my bullion concession who were willing to pay an outrageous price for my watery, yellowish liquid. These were not my fellow citizens but people from outside. I noticed that nearly all of them carried folded brochures which either extruded from their pockets or were grasped in their hands. One of these was left behind on the counter that fronted my kiosk, and I read it as soon as business slowed down. The cover of the brochure bore the words "Have a Fun Time in Funny Town." Inside were several captioned photographs of the various "attractions" that our town had to offer to the curious tourist. I was in awe of the town manager's scheme. Not only had this faceless person taken our last penny to finance the most extensive construction project the town had ever seen, from which there was no doubt a considerable amount of kickback involved, but this ingenious boondoggle had additionally brought an unprecedented flood of revenue into our town.

Yet the only one who truly prospered was the town manager. Daily, sometimes hourly, collections were made at each of the town's attractions and concessions. These were made by solemn-faced strangers who carried weapons. In addition, I noticed that spies had been integrated among the tourists, just to insure that none of us withheld more than the meager allotment of the profits that derived from the town's new enterprise. Nonetheless, whereas we had once had reason to expect nothing more than humiliation and total impoverishment under the governance of the town manager, it now appeared that we would at least survive.

One day, however, the crowds of tourists began to thin out. In short order, the town's new business had dwindled to nothing. The solemn-faced men no longer bothered to make their collections, and we began to fear the worst. Hesitantly, we began to emerge from our places and gathered together on Main Street under a sagging banner that read "Welcome to Funny Town."

"I think that's it," said Ritter, who was still wearing his bathroom attendant's uniform.

"Only one way to be sure," said Leeman, now back in adult clothes.

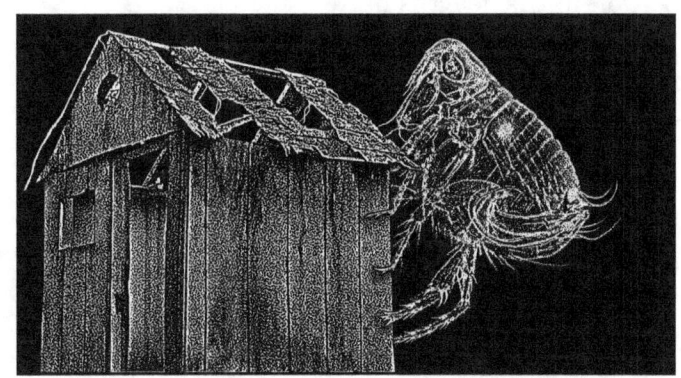

Once again we tramped out to the countryside under a gray sky some weeks before the onset of winter. It was approaching dusk, and long before we reached the town manager's shed we could see that no reddish light glowed inside. Nevertheless, we searched the shed. Then we searched the farmhouse. There was no town manager. There was no money. There was nothing.

When the rest of them turned away and began to head back to town, I stayed behind. Another town manager would arrive before long, and I did not with to see what form the new administration would take. This was the way it had always been. First the one came and then the other, each of them exhibiting signs of greater degeneracy than the one before, as if they were festering away into who knows what, just as each day in that town was more dismal than the one before. And there was no telling where it would all end. How many others would come and go, taking with them more and more of the place where I had been born and was beginning to grow old? I thought about how different that place had been when I was a child. I thought about my youthful dream of having a home in The Hill district. I thought about my old delivery business.

Then I walked in the opposite direction from the town. I walked until I came to a road. And I walked down that road until I came to another town. I passed through many towns, as well as large cities, doing clean-up work and odd jobs to keep myself going. All of them were managed according to the same principles as my old home town, although I came upon none that had reached such an advanced stage of degeneracy. I had fled that place in hopes of finding another that had been founded upon different principles and operated under a different order. But there was no such place, or none that I could find. It seemed the only course of action left to me was to make an end of it.

Not long after realizing the aforementioned facts of my existence, I was sitting at the counter of a crummy little coffee shop. It was late at night, and I was eating soup. I was also thinking about how I might make an end of it. The coffee shop may have been in a small town or a large city. Now that I think of it, the place stood beneath a highway overpass, so it must have been the latter. The only other customer in the place was a well-dressed man sitting at the other end of the counter. He was drinking a cup of coffee and, I noted, directing a sidelong glance at me every so often. I turned my head toward him and gave him a protracted stare. He smiled and asked if he could join me at my end of the counter.

"You can do whatever you like. I'm leaving."

"Not just yet," he said as sat down at the counter stool next to mine. "What business are you in?"

"None in particular. Why?"

"I don't know. You just seem like someone who knows his way around. You've been some places, am I right?"

"I suppose so," I said.

"I thought as much. Look, I am not just interested in chit-chat here. I work on commission finding people like you. And I think you've got what it takes."

"For what?" I asked.

"Town management," he replied.

I finished off the last few spoonfuls of my soup. I wiped my mouth with a paper napkin. "Tell me more," I said.

It was either that or make an end of it. Ω

VILLANELLE BY MOONLIGHT

I have roamed as long as the world is wide,
carrying bone-deep secrets in my skin.
(A wolf in the heart is hard to hide.)

I cannot fight fate while moonlight marks the tide.
Let one pale thread meet my eyes and change begins.
I have roamed as long as the world is wide.

This time I thought to see the odds defied;
I have you here and more, I call you friend
(but a wolf in the heart) is hard to hide.

Shall I speak truth — utter no more lies? I
wear two faces; one wields a killer's grin.
I have roamed as long as the world is wide.

Draw back the drapes; my hunger waits outside.
It's not a matter of "if" but "when."
(A wolf) in the heart is hard to hide.

What burns in my blood will not be denied;
Month after month the wildness filters in.
I have roamed as long as the world is wide.
A wolf in the heart is hard to hide.

— **Lane Robins**

TWO SHOWS DAILY

by Tim W. Burke

illustrated by Allen Koszowski

A smoke juggler herded his ghostly menagerie out the auditorium entrance and past me. Applause swelled for his performance. I fidgeted by the entrance until the house lights began to dim, then I entered the concealing gloom. The sparse orchestra struck a flourish; The opening burlesques were about to begin. At the far side of the theater, a baby cried. The fashionable mother of the infant passed the tiny bundle to a young usherette, who took it to the back to comfort it. Before the theater fell completely dark, I read the ticket and saw that it was only one seat in from the aisle. I stood staring at the slip of paper in the dark, frozen. A pall seemed to clear from my mind. Standing there in the dark, hearing the flourish and then a baby's cries; it all seemed somehow familiar.

Life had been impossible since my breakdown, and since I had tried to harm myself. My mind had been a blur for weeks, and I had been filled with all sorts of dreamings. Indeed, I barely remember my doctor having given me this ticket with the admonishment, "Watch the show. It will be good for you to get among people. You do want to get better, don't you?" From the back of the theater came a voice, "This way, sir. I'll help you to your seat." From the dark came a tall, burly usher. He grabbed my elbow.

My nerves jumped. I fumbled at the pocket of my coat and touched the cold single-shot pistol. I thought, *The usher's just doing his job! Steady!* I flicked my hand out of my pocket and adjusted my thick ascot. I rued bringing the pistol; in it I had imagined comfort and safety, but now saw my nerves could cause some poor innocent dire harm.

The usher led me to my aisle. We stood at the edge. There was something about the half-lit row of people that brought a gout of fear. "Your seat, sir," the usher said, strangely loud, glancing at the other patrons as if something was amiss. They seemed like rows of cadavers, the way they stared forward as one. I fought an urge to flee. The usher stared, as if prompting me for a line in a play, "Your seat. Sir."

I could hesitate and delay no more. I resigned myself, braced my nerves and plunged in. Fate tweaked me and I stepped on the toes of the puffy, taffeta-wrapped matron who was seated on the aisle. Anxious to almost trembling, I begged her sincerest pardon and fell into my seat. I looked to the stage. Another brash sting from the orchestra made up for loudness what it lacked in members. I knew from my own failures to get acting work that theaters didn't pay quality performers a decent wage. It's cheaper to pay for the lurid, and the masses love the lurid. The unions are no help, not when abominations and even the reanimated dead are now considered sport. The chime organ and brass pixiepipe struck up the lively old ditty "Saunter To The Dance Floor."

My guts chilled. I thought, *Please don't let it be . . .*

Upon the orange-lit curtain writhed huge white letters, projected from behind by a Livid Lantern: *THE GENTEEL GHOUL.*

An anguished groan escaped my lips. The matron beside me snuffled into her handkerchief.

I wanted to scream, *What is wrong with you — with this world — that you tolerate horrors like this?*

But that would have been my anxiety speaking. I was the one who was ailing and out of step. It wasn't they who were cruel, but I who was too nervous. It was so wearying to keep that always in mind. I smiled weakly, "I thought this act got old a long time ago." The old peahen said nothing. Something about how the orange light struck her made me anxious. Did I know her from an audition? No. She looked familiar, and her disdain was obvious. I turned back to the stage and gripped the arms of the seat. The wood creaked.

"The Genteel Ghoul" has been a burlesque stand-by for years. Why audiences enjoy "The Genteel Ghoul" always has been a source of mystery and disgust to me. A spotlight lit the stage, which now seemed far too close. I was conscious, so fatally conscious, of the weight of the terrible, comforting machine of destruction in my coat pocket.

Slowly, the light swung up a side promenade leading from the stage. It settled on the dark wooden doors. The doors opened and the performers entered. That these were featured performers who toured the nation, and who would be paid handsomely for *this!*

The scenario was as I remembered from countless

viewings: the lady playing the tamer was a beautiful, tiny brunette with high cheekbones and cascading hair. Her large blue eyes shone in the light. Her bare arms glowed like ivory. She was sheathed, as always, in an evening gown cut deeply to show ample cleavage. The gown's classic design was made even more fashionable by its color of deep autumnal orange, and that it was made from some sort of delicately tanned hide. Its ripples around her slim hips were at turns erotic, yet also disquieting as it suddenly made me think of a huge worm swallowing her. Her lips were frozen in a smile up at her companion.

The ghoul was stretched painfully to a fully erect posture. As always, he was dressed at the height of respectable fashion, with a suit so tailored that his hunched back was scarcely noticeable. The yellow of the suit seemed even more set off by the flaccid gray of the ghoul's skin. A stylish matching fez nestled on his scaly head down to his long, pointed ears. Blue-lensed glasses perched on his sloping snout, which provided no protection for his blinking, rolling black eyes. His jaw flexed and revealed glistening brown fangs as long as my fingers. The ghoul and the lady walked down the promenade and past the freshly plastered wall to the stage, upon which a mock theater box had now been wheeled. The tamer's shoulders flexed and swelled noticeably once as she steadied her escort's ungainly lurch.

Once upon the stage, the ghoul swatted aside the door to the mock theater box to give his lady entrance. Awkwardly, he bowed to allow her to sit on the lustrous wood, and he staggered to his seat beside her. He collapsed into his chair panting with relief.

The audience applauded loudly, also relieved. The hulking ghoul worked his terrible, wet mouth in absent search for something to bite.

The woman playing the tamer smiled and met the gaze of individuals in the crowd with gracious acknowledgements. The ghoul scrabbled after accessories, which had been set on the box railing. He opened a tin of snuff and pretended to partake. He opened a box of taffies and offered some to his lady. He consulted the evening's playbill and stroked his chin, which caused some amusement in the crowd. As he set the playbill down on the box's railing, I noticed that one tightening claw had pierced the paper like a knife blade.

Suddenly, the cold gray claw snatched up and sent the playbill flicking away. The ghoul grasped the woman's tiny hand. He slowly turned his head to her and with great formality, leaned to her ear. The ghoul's face suddenly twitched into an expression of lovelorn yearning. The creature feigned to whisper a declaration to the lady. She flushed and turned an embarrassed, succulent shoulder to her lover's maw.

Ghouls feast on the dead famously, but the living satisfy them as well.

Gently and lingeringly, he pushed his lips past his fangs. He kissed her shoulder. A shudder ran through him.

Too dramatically, she rose and pretended umbrage. The ghoul cast his wrist across his eyes and faked despair.

And throughout this abomination, I glanced fearfully at a box beside the stage. Lit by the glow of the spotlight, a plump and balding man squirmed, in a sheen of sweat. His gaze pierced the ghoul and whatever motion the man made, the ghoul followed. Did he — the real tamer — perform his feat through hypnosis like some tamers do? Or through terrible alchemistries that enslave the subject's will, even its very life, as other tamers I have heard? By my sanity, I do not know. The first requires an iron will; the latter needs but the right participant and chemicals. The true tamer perspired and strained and wrenched and glared with hollow eyes reddened by the audience's pipe tobacco and his own crushing performance. But no one noticed him as the lady on the stage asked if someone had a small child that she could borrow.

The usherette came forward with the baby. The squalling bundle of meat was handed on stage to the false tamer, who then handed it to the ghoul. The ghoul turned and cradled the screaming infant in his long fingers.

My hand found its way into my coat pocket and clutched the deadly iron device within. It had but one bullet, but I still found comfort.

Then the house lights came up. The lady waved and the music swelled signaling that the act was at long last, blessedly finished. The ghoul rose and shambled to the exit, baby still bawling in the cradle of his elbow.

Visibly startled, the lady crept next to the ghoul. She waved again, and looked meaningfully at the ghoul. The ghoul pushed her aside and continued his shamble to the door. The ghoul refused to return the baby! Everyone knew that the ghoul was supposed to return the baby! The lady looked to the true tamer, her beautiful features paling. A murmur of surprise and dismay swept the audience.

My free hand fluttered to my face. Now at last! After all these years of letting this menace be performed! The baby cried louder from the ghoul's elbow. Shouts erupted from the audience. A woman shrieked.

I will stop this! I have the means! I have the will!

But I sat frozen in horror.

Then the ghoul stopped. He turned back to the audience. And handed the infant to the usherette as he wagged his finger to the crowd as if to say, "Had you going there, didn't I?"

Of course they had to come up with some new twist . . .

Strangely, strangely, I don't know why, but that's when I stood and shrieked. I raised the pistol from my pocket.

Then I stopped. All faces were turned to me in alarm and dismay. The lady tamer, the false tamer, looked at me with anticipation. All of this, my standing, the pistol raised, seemed suddenly so familiar. I caught my sanity at this last possible moment.

"I . . . I apolo—"

Something smacked me in the back of the head. I turned. The old taffeta matron swung her purse again and caught me in my ear. She grabbed the hand that held the pistol and wrestled with its grip. Her puffing cheeks were spackled with make-up.

I pulled the trigger. I saw the white flash and felt the explosion in my hand and felt another, different electric memory resonate under my chin through my skull. The mad harridan flogged me over and over again with her surprisingly heavy handbag. The pistol only held one bullet. In some frantic, timid geometry, my aim could not decide between the three culprit performers. The bullet passed, I knew not where, as if it hadn't even existed.

The audience roared with delight as I was grabbed by three brawny ushers and the house manager. They lifted me off my feet as I struggled and cried and the matron beat me mercilessly.

I was carried out of the auditorium to great gales of laughter. Slack-faced, the ghoul waved stiffly and exited with the lady to thunderous applause.

The applause was still deafening as the doors slammed shut behind them.

I was hustled back through the lobby, brushing past a torture impressionist shrieking his vocal warm-ups. Everything was moving so quickly, and my state was so hysterical, I watched all in detached shock.

We passed I glimpsed the parlor mirror outside the lounges. A group of ushers hustled a man whose skin was waxy like the embalmed dead.

Giddy, I thought, *A corpse offended by a ghoul's performance? Call that a twist! Call that entertainment!* I was dragged to a tiny room lined with mops and brooms. There sat my doctor, smoking a cigarette, his shirt-sleeves rolled up. I was so relieved at the sight of him, I ceased my futile struggling and relaxed onto the metal table I was laid upon. He opened up my shirt and pulled off my ascot. He felt under my jaw and his fingers seemed to slip into my skin. I coughed and fumbled after his fingers. With trembling hands, I felt a large, stitched wound. My doctor slapped my hands aside and stabbed a long rubber tube up through the wound and deep, deep into my skull. He joined the free end of the tube to a bottle of fluid. Layers of black and green tendrils swirled and intermingled within the bottle like smoke. He turned to the door, where the manager was hustling the ushers out the door to their duties.

The manager said to my doctor, "Old Mary-Velle said that sitting next to him is getting to be a chore. He's starting to get ripe."

He clicked off the light out to blessed, concealing darkness. The door hinges squealed. The light from the doorway narrowed and was stirred by their shadows.

My doctor's voice echoed in the hallway, "It'll be fine, sir. We'll just use jasmine cologne."

"And he missed his cue again! How is it that he's hesitating? Third show this week —"

"Uh. It must be something in the mix. He'll be fine for next show. Look, I'll take ten percent off the monthly rate, till I can replace him. It's still cheaper than —"

The door shut with a bang. The darkness seeped into my brain, drop by drop, blurring my terror into forgetfulness, until there was only darkness, and all receded into gloom. Ω

GOOD NEIGHBORS

by Jamie Ferguson

"Susie says you're a witch." The little girl tossed her hair back over her shoulder, golden glints bright in the summer sunshine.

Mary smiled. "What an odd thing for her to say." She smoothed the fabric of her skirt, brushing off a stray leaf.

The girl pursed her lips briefly, then squirmed in her chair. She swung her legs, little feet hanging high off the floor. "Do you have a broomstick?" she asked hopefully.

Mary laughed. "I have a broom, but so do you. Does that make *you* a witch?"

"Hmmm." The little face looked disappointed.

A woman's laugh echoed through the back door. Mary looked at the door for a moment, then settled more comfortably in her chair. The porch was a much nicer place to be than the house; the sun hung low in the sky, the breeze was warm, and the neighbors . . . well, the neighbors were inside. It was nice to meet the other people on the block, but nicer to enjoy the lovely summer evening. And the girl . . . she was adorable. Quite a charming little creature. She sat slightly crooked, legs dangling from the seat, small fingers playing with the ends of her hair. "Why do you want me to be a witch?" Mary asked.

The girl scrunched her eyes up briefly, then tilted her head. "'Cause then you could do magic spells and I could fly and stuff. Of course, you'd have to be a *good* witch." She paused. "If you were a bad witch you might eat me or something. I wouldn't like *that*."

"I see. I suppose that would be less fun for you than for me."

"Yeah!" the girl agreed. "I think you should be a good witch." She looked at Mary expectantly.

"Well . . . how would you know? What if I was a bad witch and pretended to be good? Is there a way you could tell?"

The girl looked thoughtful. "I guess not."

"Tanya?" The child's mother opened the back door. "There you are. I asked you not to bother our guests." Her voice was brittle, hard; her hair and makeup, flawless.

Tanya slid out of her chair, landing on her feet with a small thump. "Okay," she said. She turned to Mary. "It was very nice talking with you," she said politely, then scampered inside.

"I hope she hasn't been too much of a pest," the mother said. "I told her not to disturb the guests." She held a dish towel in one perfectly manicured hand, long, narrow fingers wrapped tightly around it.

"Oh, no bother, no bother at all. She's a sweet thing, a pleasure to talk to," Mary replied.

"Well, that's good," the woman replied. "I'd better get inside and finish putting out the food."

"I'll be right in then, thank you," Mary said. The other woman smiled, a tight, thin smile, then hurried back inside. Not a friendly woman, certainly nothing like her daughter. The daughter . . . now, she was a delight. Bright, inquisitive, and quite a fetching personality. Definitely a child to see again.

Mary went over to the chair the girl had been sitting in and looked at it for a moment, then smiled. She picked up several pieces of hair, long, golden strands. Ah yes, there was a third one. Perfect. She folded them carefully in a napkin, tucked it in her bag, then straightened up and went to join the rest of the party. It was always good to get to know your neighbors. Ω

ILLUSTRATED LIMERICK

A streetwalker — pretty, but daft —
(Well, those in the know kind of laughed)
   Was looking — no fooling
    To further her schooling;
The major she planned was Lovecraft.

                — George Barr

BIZARREMOST BAZAAR

Third eyes, a mere five crystal coins,
although a length of those lovely
silver tentacles would surely be a fair trade —
a final bit of garnish for this crawling cloak.
Aye, madame, thank you, and the eye —
Yes, a most creative placement indeed,
an accent that winks back from the very place
the male gaze is most drawn. Madame,
my compliments . . .

             The skin here,
freshly shed from the finest of farm-spawned
salamanders — see, slip it on, how snug fits
this glove, feel the fire ball in your hand
as you crook your fingers — just take care
not to scratch, or rub your eyes . . .

                This skull,
reassembled, cleaned and spiritually cleansed
from the most exclusive of exhumed royalty's
remains — perhaps even an ancestor, venerable
sir? Certainly perfect, you must agree, for
replacing that moldering jaw and giving
your poor, exposed brain some needed protection . . .

These jars, here? Only the wealthiest
of the wealthy can afford these, or need them.
Stray souls captured in the slipstream
where Time's friction warms the astral sphere.
There is no way to tell, in this rawest form,
what these wriggling mites might have been
among the living, saints, despots, worms,
behemoths, mightiest of stars or
a thoughtless rock slowly wearing away —
but even you, my friend, must admit
the gamble is far better than ending
this existence with no soul at all . . . .

— **Mike Allen**

ILLUSTRATED LIMERICK

The love, with whom each night I sup,
And drink from the same golden cup,
    Each day grows more fair;
    So why should I care
If the sand in her hourglass runs *up?*
        — **George Barr**

MAEVE

by Lillian Csernica

illustrated by George Barr

The car gave one last churning rattle and rolled to a stop. John Fenton turned on the ignition. The engine made a noise like a spoon dropped into a garbage disposal. He checked his oil gauge. The red warning light glared. The pressure was low. When he first turned on the engine and listened to it in the rental agency's lot, he'd thought the car could stand a quart or two. The agent assured him it was just a cold engine on a foggy morning. He sat back and closed his eyes. If he started screaming, whoever heard him would likely have him arrested as a lunatic.

He had maybe an hour of daylight left. Where he'd find a garage way out here in the Irish countryside he had no idea. Smaller lanes and dirt tracks led off the main road he followed, but aside from the occasional barn or cluster of cows he didn't see anything promising. The cows huddled together as though they didn't like being stranded there either. He'd heard they did that right before it rained. That was true, to judge from the clouds massing on the western horizon. They promised an impressive storm. Frustration made him thump the steering wheel. All he needed was to get caught in a downpour hiking along in search of a tow truck.

John got out and walked toward a paved side lane that looked well used. He'd been on the lane about fifteen minutes when a battered pickup pulled alongside him and slowed to match his pace. A bearded face with a cap drawn low over the eyes leaned out of the driver's window.

"That your motor back there?"

John nodded.

"Thought so. Conked out on you, did it?" The man jerked a thumb at the bed of the pickup. "Jump in the back. I'll give you a lift."

"Thanks." John climbed in over the side and the pickup lurched forward. Around the next bend they entered a village. The pickup slowed to a stop beside two ancient gas pumps. Next to them stood a weather-beaten garage. John jumped down as the driver got out.

"Can you point me to the mechanic?" John asked.

"You're looking at him. David Neeson." They shook hands. "Any idea what the trouble is?"

"Oil, maybe the coolant system. It rattled a lot."

Neeson nodded. "I'll have a look at it after I finish here. There's a pub across the way." He looked up at the sky. "You'll not want to wait out in the open."

"I sure don't." John looked around. "Where is everyone?"

"They're in the pub, like as not."

"Everybody? Is it bingo night or something?"

Neeson glanced up at the darkening clouds. "Looks like one of Maeve's nights."

"Who's she?"

Neeson shrugged. "Hard to say. Folks say some fishermen found her sitting on the beach one morning after a bad storm. Just a little thing she was then, barely school age."

"The police couldn't find her parents?"

Neeson shook his head. "And no one came forward asking for her, either. A local family took her in, raised her normal enough. Still. . . ." He looked up at the crescent moon shining through a gap in the clouds. "My old Gran said she once knew of a child born of a man and a selkie. It came out human-legged, so the selkie tribe threw it ashore to die. Makes you wonder, eh?" He climbed back into the truck. "Go on, now. I'll stop in later."

"Thanks again." John walked across the lane to the fieldstone building whose hanging sign read **The Haven**. When he opened the door the good smells of beef stew and stout wafted out. He took a stool at the bar. A dark-haired man with a broad, honest face came down the bar to him.

"What'll you have?"

"A pint of Guinness."

The barkeep set the pint of front of him.

John handed over two pound notes. The barkeep kept his eyes on John as he counted out the change.

"American, are you?"

"That's right."

"You're far off the path to come to Droghlow."

"My car broke down out on the highway."

"You'll want to see the man across the way. He's the mechanic hereabouts."

Before John could say he already had, the barkeep stepped away to serve a man and woman who'd just come in. It was only Tuesday, but they wore what had to be their Sunday best. The woman even had on a bonnet and gloves, the man a tie. They took their pints to a table and sat side by side, watching the door.

John looked around the room. Aside from the bar-maids, everyone there was dressed up. For some of the men it meant little more than a combing of their hair and beards and wearing their best shirts. The women in particular were turned out at their best. Most of them had some small bundle with them, carried in a basket or wrapped in a shawl.

A man sat by himself in the far corner. From the number of wet rings on the table and the foam on his black mustache, the man must have been drinking hard for the last hour. He hunched over his pint as though someone was about to snatch it from him. The man's surly look made John suspect he'd welcome cause for a fight.

The door blew open. A woman cried out. A glass fell off a table and shattered. In the doorway stood Neeson the mechanic. The wind howled around him.

"Shut that door!" Bill yelled.

"I'm looking for the Yank."

"Here I am." John raised his glass, then wished he hadn't. Everyone in the pub stared at him. Their surprise gave way to disapproval and worse. Neeson made his way through the crowd to the bar.

"You'll need a part I can't find short of Waterford."

"Can you get there and back tonight?" John asked.

Neeson shook his head. "Getting across the lane was trouble enough. You'll have to stay over."

"Dave." Bill stood nearby. "He'll not find a room anywhere tonight. Haven't you got a motor he can use?"

"None that runs."

Bill rubbed a hand across his face. "You've got to do something. We can't have him here!"

"And I can't wave a wrench over the bloody thing and make it fix itself." Neeson turned back to John. "I'll hitch it to my lorry and bring it into the garage. You can call for it there after noon."

"Where can I get a room?"

Neeson nodded at Bill. "Ask him. He'll be your landlord." He ducked out, dragging the door shut after him.

John looked at Bill. Bill sighed, then leaned his elbows on the bar and waved John closer. "Look, mate, you've caught us on a bad night. I'd love to oblige, but as you can see, we're full up."

"Really. All these people are tourists who've booked every room for tonight?"

"I'm trying to make this easy on you. Just go. Please. There's a barn every other mile out there. You can bed down in the hay."

"Are you serious?" John looked out the window at the flashes of lightning that were all that pierced the blackness. "You'd send me out into that weather, even though I can pay?"

While they were talking, a woman wearing a stained apron over her plain blue dress came out of the door behind the bar. She fussed with the pins holding her fair hair in a bun. A few curls straggled down her neck. "Bill, we've still got the little room next to the attic."

"Hush, Kate. Get back in the kitchen."

John pulled out two 10-pound notes, watched Kate's eyes widen. He pulled out two more. It wasn't just the room. He wanted to know what these people were waiting for, and why they were doing everything they could to make sure he wasn't around for it.

"Bill." Kate stepped out to take his arm. "We can't send him away. It's not right."

"You want him here when she comes? A stranger, not even Irish?"

A fierce wind whipped down the lane, rattling the shutters and blowing leaves and gravel against the windowpanes. Another gust hit the door like a fist and blew it inward. In the doorway stood a girl little more than seventeen. She was barefoot. Her jeans and blouse were plastered to her with rain and mud. Her eyes were fixed on some point in the air. They reminded John of lit windows in an empty house. The strangest part was her hair. Messy as she was in every other way, her long brown hair hung over her shoulder in a neat braid.

Kate closed her eyes and let out a long sigh. "Thank God."

The level of conversation surged, pushed upward by back-slapping, happy smiles, and several calls for another round. The girl walked straight over to a little table by the window and sat with her back to the wall. Kate hurried round the end of the bar toward her, then slowed to a careful walk as she came near.

"Evening, Maeve. Anything I can get you? Anything at all?"

Maeve stared out at nothing. A little smile bent her lips. "I'll sit awhile, if that's all right."

"Whatever you like." Kate's smile and cheerful tone didn't match the way her hands knotted her apron. She rushed back to the bar and Bill.

"You did well, love." He put his arm around her. "You always do."

"She's a dear girl. It's just — I was so afraid she'd come in all tangled up!"

John watched the crowd. People glanced at each other, looked away. The women tidied their bundles and sat forward, looking edgy. At last one woman pulled her coat tight around her and stood up. She kept her head high and carried her basket over to where Maeve sat. John saw brief smiles and nods follow her, salutes to the woman's courage. He was dying to ask what all this was about. The grim look on Bill's face and the protective way he held Kate told John not to bother him. The woman reached Maeve's table.

"Evening, Maeve."

"Evening, Fiona."

"Would you have a moment, dear? I don't want to trouble you."

That eerie smile pulled Maeve's lips upward. "No trouble at all, Fiona."

Fiona perched on the edge of the chair across from Maeve. "My little Charlotte was lucky enough to have two of the lads come courting at the same time. Well, the poor girl won't listen to any reason. Mark Randall is a good boy, but he's not got half the future of the Flynn's boy Terry. I just don't know what to do with her. Love's well and good, but she's got to think about —"

"Fiona."

The room got quiet. People looked everywhere but at Maeve. Still, it was plain they hung on her every word.

"An empty bed is better than a lonely one with two people in it."

"You mean — I should let Charlotte follow her heart?"

"What do you want more? A happy child with lots of happy babies, or a rich child who cries at night?"

Fiona's lip quivered. She put her hands to her eyes. When she spoke again, her voice shook. "Bless you, Maeve. I see the way of it now." She reached into her basket and took out a loaf wrapped in a tea towel. "I thought you might like a bit of my soda bread. You enjoyed it so much when you were over for tea."

"Thank you, Fiona."

Fiona set the loaf on the table and hurried back to her own seat, dabbing at her eyes. Another woman rose and went to sit before Maeve.

"Evening, Maeve."

"Evening, Grace."

"It's my brother Kevin. He moons about pale as a ghost. Won't eat, sleeps too much, won't say a word to save his life. Neither the doctor nor the priest can do a thing for him."

"Let him go, Grace. His heart's too big for a little village. It pinches and chafes."

"But he's my only kin! If he goes, who'll be left?"

"Let him go, Grace. He'll come back to you and bring a family with him. He'll need your help with the babies."

Grace's mouth fell open. In her expression was a hope so desperate it pained John to see it. "You mean it? Babies?"

"The sooner you let him go the more there's likely to be."

Grace left a fine wooden comb on the table. Others came and went, each leaving some little gift. John kept his eyes on his pint but strained to hear every word. He might have been sitting in the confessional. These people poured out their greatest pains to Maeve, yet she seemed to know even more about their troubles than they did. Each went away comforted, if not a good deal happier. Through it all Maeve sat there staring at nothing, her eyes alight with that empty glow.

The logical part of John's mind fought to deny what he was seeing. It was a little village. Everyone knew everyone else's secrets. Maybe the storm did kick loose some sensitivity in Maeve, but what she told them was probably nothing more than common sense mixed with unselfish compassion. He grinned.

Some lawyer he was. No matter how he argued, he couldn't convince himself, couldn't argue down the urge to ask her about his own troubles. Even the smallest shred of hope would make going home more bearable.

He'd come to Ireland the day before yesterday, having arrived in England a week earlier. The trip was a present from his father to congratulate them both on John passing the bar.

Dad wanted him to go see where the family had started generations back, so he could appreciate how far they'd come. There was the unspoken expectation that he'd return to New York full of gratitude and family pride. Just the right attitude to carry on the Fenton name as a junior partner in the family law practice. He'd spent the last four years staring that fate in the face.

While John enjoyed the complicated puzzle of getting both sides of the story and resolving a case, the lust for victory obvious in the stories his father and uncle told struck him as more appropriate to professional wrestling than to the court room. He had less than a week of freedom left before his indentured servitude began. Now all he wanted to do was run like hell.

He tapped Bill on the arm. "Would she talk to me?"

"You! I told you —"

"Listen to me! I have a problem too. It will make all the difference in my life to know the answer to it."

Bill glared at him. "You're serious? You're not looking for some funny story to tell the folks back home?"

"No! Please, I can't tell you how important this is. What she tells me could save my life."

Bill looked down at Kate where she huddled against him. "Do we trust him, love?"

Kate sized John up with a wary eye. "Tell us your problem."

"I want to know if I should go back home to my father, to join his business."

She studied him for a long moment, then nodded. "Wait till I call you, then be quick."

Another woman walked away from Maeve's table. By now it was covered with gifts. Maeve leaned her head against the windowpane. The weird light in her eyes had dulled.

Kate stopped at the end of the bar and looked all around the room. No one else stood up. She beckoned John. He slid off the stool. Bill caught his sleeve.

"You'll need to take her something."

John looked over at Maeve's pale cheeks and lips. "A small brandy. She looks like she needs it."

With a nod Bill fetched it. He held it back from John's reaching hand. "I warn you. You do anything to upset her and we'll send you home in a box."

Kate walked John over to Maeve's table. Mutters of shock and disapproval followed him. John ignored them and sat down.

"Good evening, Miss."

A puzzled look replaced Maeve's smile. "I don't know you."

"I'm John Fenton. I need your help." He thought hard, trying to phrase the question so the answer would do him the most good. "When I go home, I'll have to join my father's firm. If I don't go home, I don't know what I'll do. Do I have any other choices?"

She stared over his shoulder. The light in her eyes brightened. "You took your father's money. Now you've got to do the job you've been paid for."

"It's not like that!"

"Isn't it? Your father paid you to be what he wants

you to be. If you back out now, you'll not be the man you want yourself to be."

Anger and embarrassment flushed his face. She'd struck right to the ugly core of it. For a moment John just sat there, impaled by the cold truth. Then he took a deep breath. If this was the public confessional, he'd confess all.

"He treats me like I'm a hired hand, like some new piece of equipment he bought for the office! I'm not a person to him, I'm just another damned trophy! If I go back to that, I won't be what I want myself to be then either."

"What do you want to be? In that office, and in your heart?"

John opened his mouth to answer. No words came out. Nothing even came to mind, aside from a vague picture of himself running from his father's grasping hands. "I don't know."

"Then I'll tell you what you need. You need guts enough to stand up to your father and tell him what his money cannot buy. He cannot buy spare parts to build the son he dreams of. You are the son he has. He must love you as you are."

John's breath hitched. He looked away from the piercing light in her eyes. Now he knew why only the women spoke to Maeve. It was no shame for them to cry in public. He set the brandy glass before her.

"You look cold. I thought you might like this."

"Thank you, John."

He started to rise. Kate gasped. Maeve's hand reached out to grasp the brandy glass and press it to her lips. She sipped. Her eyes closed. A faint blush colored her cheeks. Her smile looked genuine. John looked at Kate, wondering if he'd done something wrong.

"She's never done that before," Kate whispered. "She always leaves her gifts till tomorrow, after she wakes up."

Across the room a chair fell over with a crash.

"Right! I've had enough of this!" It was the man with a black mustache, the one John had caught staring at him. "All the time she's been here, never once has she said a word to me or my woman. Won't look at us, won't talk to us, won't even fetch us our ale when we come in. She'll talk to a Yank but she won't talk to her own!"

"Now you listen here, Harry Doolittle," Bill said. "Pay your tab and get yourself home."

"If I don't?"

"You know better, Harry. Pay me later. Just get out!"

Doolittle threw his arms wide. "Look at you, all of you! Afraid of a little girl who runs out in the storm like some daft deer. She comes in with that rope of hair all pretty and you all sing her praises." He bot-

tomed the last of his latest pint and slammed it down on the table. "Remember when she came in looking like a banshee with her hair blown into knots? The next day old Murphy's barn burned. It's not right, I tell you! It's time we put an end to it!" He pulled a fillet knife from his belt. "I'll have that braid off and we'll be free of her at last!"

Bill swept the glasses out of his way and heaved himself over the bar. "Mike! Danny!"

Two men behind Doolittle leaped up and grabbed his arms. Bill rushed over to pry the knife from his hand.

"You get the hell out of here and don't let me see your face again!"

Doolittle thrashed in their grip as the three men hauled him toward the door.

"She'll talk to those she likes but it's the back of her for the rest of us! She even let a Yank buy her a drink! I say she's a fake!"

Shocked silence choked the whole room. Bill's face flushed a deep red.

"Get him out of here before he gets hurt."

Shouts of agreement, threats, and outrage shattered the silence. The men hustled Harry to the door. Above the noise rose one singular voice.

"Let him be." Maeve raised her head. Her smile was gone. A darker light filled her eyes. "You." She raised a limp hand to point at Doolittle. "Sit down."

Doolittle lunged toward the door. Bill grabbed him by the back of his jacket. Mike and Danny helped Bill drag Doolittle back to his chair. They slammed him down into it, then looked at Maeve. Her eyes no longer stared at empty space. They were fixed on Doolittle as she walked toward him. He strained back from her.

"I didn't mean it! Jesus God, let me go!"

Maeve sat down across from him. Doolittle shut his eyes and pulled back as far as the chair and his captors would allow.

"Please, Maeve! It's the ale, I've had too much — I'm sorry!"

Maeve untied the ribbon that bound the end of her braid and threw it on the table in front of him. Then she began unplaiting the braid. Gasps came from all sides. Kate clapped one hand to her mouth and crossed herself with the other. Bill, Mike and Danny backed away. Doolittle sat frozen in his seat, eyes wide with horror as he watched Maeve's long hair fall loose. At last it all tumbled down the front of her. She held out her hand.

"Bill. The knife."

"Maeve —"

"The knife."

Bill's hand shook as he laid the hilt of the knife across her palm. Maeve drew a length of her hair through her fingers until only an inch stuck out between them. She bent the lock of hair into a loop and slid the knife through to cut away the last inch. She held the bit of hair up to Doolittle's sweating face, then dropped it into his glass.

"Trouble for trouble, Harry Doolittle. That's all you bring and that's all you'll take with you."

She threw his knife down in front of him. The clatter snapped him out of his daze. He snatched up the knife and ran. Just as he reached the door, another violent gust of wind blew it open. He shied back, then plunged out into the storm.

Bill struggled to force the door closed against the wind. Maeve let out a long sigh. John watched the light in her eyes dim. Her head fell back and her arms hung over the sides of the chair. Kate took a step toward her, reached out a hand, drew it back.

"I — I should be getting her upstairs now. I've never seen her so tired."

"I'll have to carry her," Bill said. They both took another hesitant step toward Maeve. Kate spun around and threw herself into Bill's arms. She sobbed against his chest. No one else spoke or even moved.

John looked at the fear plain on every face. Kate had said something about tangled hair, and Doolittle had compared Maeve to a banshee. To touch her now might mean sharing the curse she'd put on Doolittle. Maeve told him he needed guts. He was already in for trouble when he stood up to his father. A little more bad luck wouldn't make much difference. He touched Bill's shoulder.

"Let me."

All heads turned toward him. Bill hugged Kate tight, his expression a mixture of confusion and that terrible fear.

"Please," John said. "Maybe this is why I'm here tonight. I'll take the bad luck with me when I go."

Bill wiped a hand across his face. He chewed at his lip, then nodded. "Go on, Katie. Show him the way."

John slid his arms under Maeve's shoulders and knees and lifted her up. Her hair hung down over his arms, almost brushing the floor. The breeze from the window caught the ends and made them float upward. The people cringed back. Some stood and jumped away to avoid the touch of Maeve's hair. The men dragged aside their tables to clear a path between John and the stairway door. Kate opened it for him and led him up the stairs.

"She lives here?" he asked.

"Works here too. She's got no family of her own."

He followed her into a small bedroom. Kate lifted an old blanket off the seat of a chair and spread it over the clean bedclothes. He laid Maeve down on it, then turned to go back downstairs. Kate laid a hand on his arm.

"I'm sorry we were harsh to you. We have to be so careful when it's one of Maeve's nights."

"Does she do this often?"

"Only on stormy nights, and only once or twice a year at that. She'll be herself come morning." Kate stood looking down at Maeve. Her smile was weary but loving.

"But — How? How does she know these things?"

"She's got the Sight. Born with a caul, like as not." Kate sighed, shaking her head. "It's a terrible gift. We're lucky to have her."

John went downstairs and took his seat at the bar. The pub had begun to empty out. As soon as Bill saw him, he hurried over.

"That was a brave thing you did." He held out his hand. John shook it. "Join me for a pint?"

"A shot of whiskey, if you don't mind. I need something stronger."

Bill set two shot glasses on the bar and reached for a bottle of Bushmill's. "You and me both."   Ω

by Lillian Csernica   37

MANILA PERIL

by Margaret L. Carter

illustrated by Allen Koszowski

When I decided to shadow my twenty-one-year-old son, I expected drugs or alcohol, not a monster. I'd left all that behind when I'd married an American naval officer and moved to San Diego. By the time my husband abandoned me by dying in a senseless accident on an aircraft carrier, I'd become used to Southern California and had no desire to return to the Philippines. Our son Jeff deserved to grow up in the culture where he felt at home. And since he looked and behaved completely human, I saw no reason to complicate his life by letting him know he might have turned out otherwise.

I got desperate enough to consider following Jeff one evening when I blocked the hallway, and he shoved past me. "You're not going to stay out half the night again, are you? You didn't even eat dinner — again."

"Quit treating me like a little kid! I'm not six years old, for Christ's sake!"

"Jeffrey George Milner, don't you dare use that kind of language to —"

You'd think two intelligent people could write a more original script.

About two weeks previously, Jeff had started oversleeping. He missed morning classes, reported to work late, even called in sick a few times because he didn't feel like getting out of bed. This, from the guy who used to be one of those disgusting sing-in-the-shower early birds. Now and then he slept through *meals,* which convinced me he really was sick. He denied it, in an unfamiliar surly tone. For his evening classes he used to ride with me sometimes, since I worked the late shift at the university library. Now he shunned me like a sulky teenager.

He stayed out every night from sunset until after midnight, without a word of explanation. *He's an adult; he doesn't have to clock in with Mom,* I kept reminding myself. Myself wasn't convinced, not when he looked downright haggard.

Finally, I cornered him as he was about to leave and demanded an explanation. All I got was a tirade. "Why don't you just mind your own business and get off my back?"

"When you're skipping classes I'm paying for, it is my —" The slam of the door cut me off. I hurried to the picture window to watch him stomp down the driveway to his shiny green compact, which I thought of as the Junebug. It squealed away from the curb and roared down the street toward the freeway.

I decided it was time to snoop. True, I could have used my special "influence" to worm answers out of him. I drew the line at doing that to my own son. Searching his room, though, fell just within my moral limits. *Too bad boys don't keep diaries.* In my favor, though, was Jeff's pack rat character. He never threw anything away except under duress. If he'd brought home any material evidence from those nocturnal wanderings, it would still be in there somewhere.

So I waded in and commenced sifting through the sedimentary layers. I didn't bother with the folded stack of clean laundry on one side of the floor. Rifling through the dirty clothes scattered over the rest of the room, along with books and CDs, I checked the pockets of all the jeans and shorts. Though Jeff has never smoked, I found a couple of matchbooks. No surprise — he started collecting them for the cover illustrations in junior high and keeps picking them up out of habit. In addition, along with wadded Kleenex and loose change, I extracted a batch of crumpled cash register receipts. Like the matchbooks, all the receipts were labeled "Manila Pearl." The latest was dated the previous day, when Jeff had stayed out until almost two A.M.

So the boy was exploring his heritage. Nothing wrong with that, as long as he stayed innocent of certain parts of that heritage. My husband had known, of course, what my nocturnal lifestyle and peculiar diet meant. He not only accepted my nature but enjoyed certain aspects of it as much as I did. Nevertheless, he'd been relieved when Jeff had turned out looking almost Anglo and completely human.

This Manila Pearl place had to be either a restaurant or a bar. Gratefully exiting the musty bedroom, I grabbed the phone book and flipped through the yellow pages. I didn't have much hope that Jeff was doing something as harmless as spending his modest salary on dinner every night. But I found the

Manila Pearl under "Restaurants," at a Chula Vista address.

Maybe he was meeting a girl? As thin as he looked, he sure wasn't stuffing himself with Filipino cuisine, which he could have done at home anytime. I had to find out what was going on, preferably without Jeff's knowing that I'd checked up on him.

Spreading a county street map on the dining room table, I located the restaurant's address. The map could protect me from getting lost but couldn't tell me what kind of neighborhood I was heading into. Chula Vista, near the Mexican border, had a rebuilt downtown of quaint shops and restaurants, a less cozy commercial district, and residential areas ranging from upscale to shabby to downright dingy. While I would fit into the ethnic ambience of the establishment more easily than my son could, if it was located in an unsavory part of town I might have to waste time and effort fending off muggers. I reassured myself that Jeff had visited the restaurant several times and lived to tell about it — or not tell about it, in his case.

Since it was dark already, I stopped dawdling, got in the car, and headed south on Interstate Five. The route I'd traced on the map led me, as I'd half expected, past downtown Chula Vista into areas of poor street lighting, trash-littered sidewalks, and decorating schemes dominated by neon and graffiti.

Twice I had to pull over and study the map to get back on track. I wondered what had ever lured Jeff down here in the first place. Finally I turned onto the proper street and caught sight of the Manila Pearl, its name on the roof in blue-violet neon letters with the bottom of the second L burned out. Slowing to a crawl, I surveyed the parking lot. Yes, there was the Junebug. I wasn't sure whether or not to feel relieved. *Depends on what he's doing here, doesn't it? This could be a drug dealers' hangout, for all I know.*

And what if it was? Should I tip off the authorities and get the place raided? No, this was a personal matter, and if a junkie got between me and my child, the cops could pick up the gory fragments later.

I drove around the block and found a parking space under one of the widely scattered street lamps. If Jeff left before I did, he wouldn't see the car.

Inside the building, the aroma of chicken adobo pervaded the air. When Jeff was little, he used to call it "chicken a-go-go." The scent of garlic wafted toward me, too. I breathed shallowly and fought a rumble of nausea. A dark-haired, olive-skinned hostess in a tight red dress greeted me. "Table for one, ma'am?"

"No, thanks, I'm just looking for a friend." I slipped past her to scan the dining room. Plastic tablecloths, candles, fake flowers, Hispanic and Oriental faces. No sign of Jeff.

"I don't see him," I said to the hostess. "Is there a separate cocktail lounge?"

"The door is around the side," she said, with a leftward wave.

I thanked her and walked around the building to the bar entrance. So if he was here, as his car indicated, he was drinking, not eating. Yet he hadn't been coming home drunk.

I stepped into the dim, shadowed cocktail lounge. On a week night, it was sparsely occupied. A baseball game played at low volume on the TV. The faint light presented no problem for my eyes. Concerned that Jeff might notice me, I paused to shroud myself in a psychic veil, a projection of *Don't notice me, I'm not really here.*

When I scanned the room, I saw him immediately, at a table up front. I'd arrived just in time, because at that moment one of the waitresses set her tray down on the end of the bar and slinked over to Jeff. He stood up and hugged her, following up with a lingering kiss. As preoccupied as he was, I might have been able to skip the "don't see me" spell.

So it is a girl! Or a woman, probably in her mid-twenties. She was surprisingly tall, almost as tall as Jeff, with *Vogue*-model legs but no breasts to speak of. She wore the same tight, scarlet, satin dress as the other female employees, with a slit to mid-thigh on one side. A thick braid of glossy, black hair hung to her waist. She had fair skin and Eurasian facial features, a poster child of the Pacific melting pot. A strange hue in her aura — I felt that she was more than she appeared, but I couldn't pin down the impression.

Now what? I could hardly storm over to the table and demand her intentions. I watched Jeff and the girl cooing to each other over drinks, a beer for him, something fruity for her. I could understand why he hadn't invited her home for dinner; he could legitimately expect me to act stuffy about his dating a cocktail waitress. What I couldn't fathom was why, contrary to his past track record with girls, his health and behavior had disintegrated. Lovesickness and sleep deprivation alone couldn't have reduced him to such a wreck. *Has she turned him on to some exotic drug? Could a chemical dependency account for the odd colors in her aura?*

A few minutes after I arrived, they finished their drinks and headed for the door, arms around each other's waists. I slipped outside, pausing at the edge of the parking lot to watch the couple. I glimpsed them as a pair of dark silhouettes next to the Junebug, leaning against the car in an embrace. After a minute of that, Jeff opened the door to let the girl in, then settled in the driver's seat and started the engine.

I considered and dismissed the idea of following them. I had a general idea of the situation and hardly needed more evidence. Instead, I went back inside and dropped my illusion of invisibility.

Perching on a bar stool, I ordered a white wine. The bartender, a short, stocky man with salt-and-pepper hair, served it and pushed a fresh basket of popcorn within reach. "Could I ask you about that waitress who just left?" I said.

"Corazon? What about her?" he said in accented English.

Yeah, what do I want to know, anyway? Whether she has drug connections? I decided to start simply, adding a psychic nudge to make him cooperative. "How long has she worked here?"

"Couple, maybe three months."

"Do you know anything about her past? I mean, where she's from, where she worked before?"

"Lady, she's legal and she never misses her shift. What else do I need to know?" He started to move down the bar.

I increased the mental pressure and switched from English to Tagalog. "Wait — I'm just wondering if she goes out with many different men."

"What are you asking all this for?" he said in the same language. "She steal your husband?" His faint smirk suggested that he figured he'd guessed right.

"No, that's my son she just left with."

The bartender's expression turned serious. "Don't worry too much about him. He's not the first, probably not the last. It never lasts long with her."

Great, now I have to worry about his heart getting broken. "I don't want him hurt — Is she married?"

"Not that I ever heard."

"What else, then?" I sensed an undercurrent of hostility, with a tinge of nervousness, in his comments.

The bartender muttered a word that sounded like — no, it couldn't be. "What did you say?"

"Danag," he repeated more distinctly.

I took a deep breath to tame the racing of my heart. "What do you know about *danag?*"

"Just a fairy tale. Nobody believes that stuff anymore. But if I did —" he glanced around and lowered his voice — "that's what I'd call her."

"Why?" I couldn't keep the sharpness from my tone.

"Bloodsucking monster, that's what she looks like. You must've heard the legends back home. Like vampires in the movies."

I reminded myself that lashing out at this superstitious fool wouldn't help my son. "Not quite like the movies."

"The story goes, they used to live with the hill folks, the Isneg tribe. The *danag* worked with them in the taro fields, and the farmers gave blood to feed them. Until the demons got carried away and started draining people to death."

"I've heard that their side of the story is a bit different. The *danag* did not become greedy; the mortals became selfish. They began refusing to donate the small amounts of blood they could easily spare. So the — others — had no choice but to take it by force." I drew a deep breath to quell my anger. "And if this girl seems not quite human, well, our people have tales of other kinds of 'vampires.' The *aswang* and the *tiyanak*, monstrous ravishers who entice and drain men without mercy —" I cut off the lecture with an impatient shake of my head. Lurid legends would always prevail over facts. Why did I waste time defending my race to this idiot? Especially when I wouldn't allow him to remember the conversation anyway.

A trace of outright fear crept into his eyes. He sidled toward the end of the bar, where one of the waitresses stood with her tray and an order slip. "I can't talk; I got work to do."

With a command for him to forget he'd met me, I ended the conversation. I hurried back to the car, my thoughts churning like a storm-racked sea. The woman who'd seduced Jeff wasn't one of my kind, but could she be something even less human?

All the rest of the night, I mulled over what Jeff's lover might be. Several possibilities, each one alarming, came to mind. I recalled the *aswang*, a birdlike night-flyer disguised as a lovely maiden by day, the *mandurugo*, whose feeding causes her many husbands to waste away and die, and the *tiyanak*, also in woman shape, draining blood with her long, hollow tongue. *This girl is just a "vamp" in the seductive sense,* I told myself, *nothing worse. That off-color streak in her aura has to come from drugs. So don't panic.* Near dawn I fell asleep mulling over the problem and dreamed of the girl, Corazon, swooping into Jeff's window on black wings, shrieking like a banshee.

I woke up groggy the next afternoon. After stumbling to the bathroom and splashing my face, I tested Jeff's doorknob. Locked, not surprisingly. But that wouldn't stop me from checking on him. I wouldn't even need to use my inhuman strength to break in. Our indoor locks, as in most recently built houses, were a joke. I shrugged on my robe, collected a miniature screwdriver from the kitchen, and broke in. The job took about five seconds.

I wasn't worried about waking Jeff. Lately, he

slept almost as heavily as one of my kind, dozing through alarm clocks, and had to be shaken for two or three minutes to force so much as a groan out of him. What more did I expect to find, anyway? Did I have some dream hangover in the back of my mind, urging me to hunt for signs of bloodsucking?

The heavily curtained bedroom, dim and stale-smelling, felt too warm. I discovered he'd closed the floor vent to cut off the flow from the air conditioner. *Come to think of it, he's been overdressing for the weather the past few days.* Another possible symptom of sickness.

Still obeying instinct rather than rational sense, I leaned over the bed and peeled Jeff's sheet down to the waist. I thought I glimpsed some marks on his bare chest. Leaning closer, I stared at them.

I sucked in my breath and swayed, grabbing the bedpost. Not the razor-like incisions he would have received from a female of my race. Tiny punctures, at least ten of them. I swallowed the snarl that threatened to rise in my throat.

What has that bloodthirsty bitch done to him?

Luckily I didn't have to work that evening. I could lurk in wait for Jeff and tell him — what? That his girlfriend was a legendary monster? From those wounds, I had a good idea of what kind, too. For the moment, though, the best I could do was try to reason with him on a more mundane level. When he staggered out of his bedroom, I intercepted him with a glass of milk, which he automatically chugged. "Weren't you supposed to have classes today? And Mr. Emory from the marina called to find out why you missed work twice in a row."

He thrust the empty glass into my hand. "I didn't feel like it."

I inventoried his appearance — damp hair, tight jeans, U.C. San Diego T-shirt, denim jacket despite the warm weather, purple shadows under his eyes despite sleeping all day. "You're not waltzing out of here this time until we have a talk." *Damn, there I go again; I have to watch that heavy parent tone of voice.*

"Save it, Mom, I'm late for an appointment."

"With Corazon?"

"Huh? Who?" The innocent pose didn't look any more convincing than it had when he'd skipped school to go to the video arcade in tenth grade.

"That witch in the slinky red dress. I know where you've been spending your nights." Instantly I wished I could delete the words. Insulting his true love wouldn't encourage him to listen to me.

A cold mask settled over his face. "You followed me. What the hell makes you think you can butt into my life that way?"

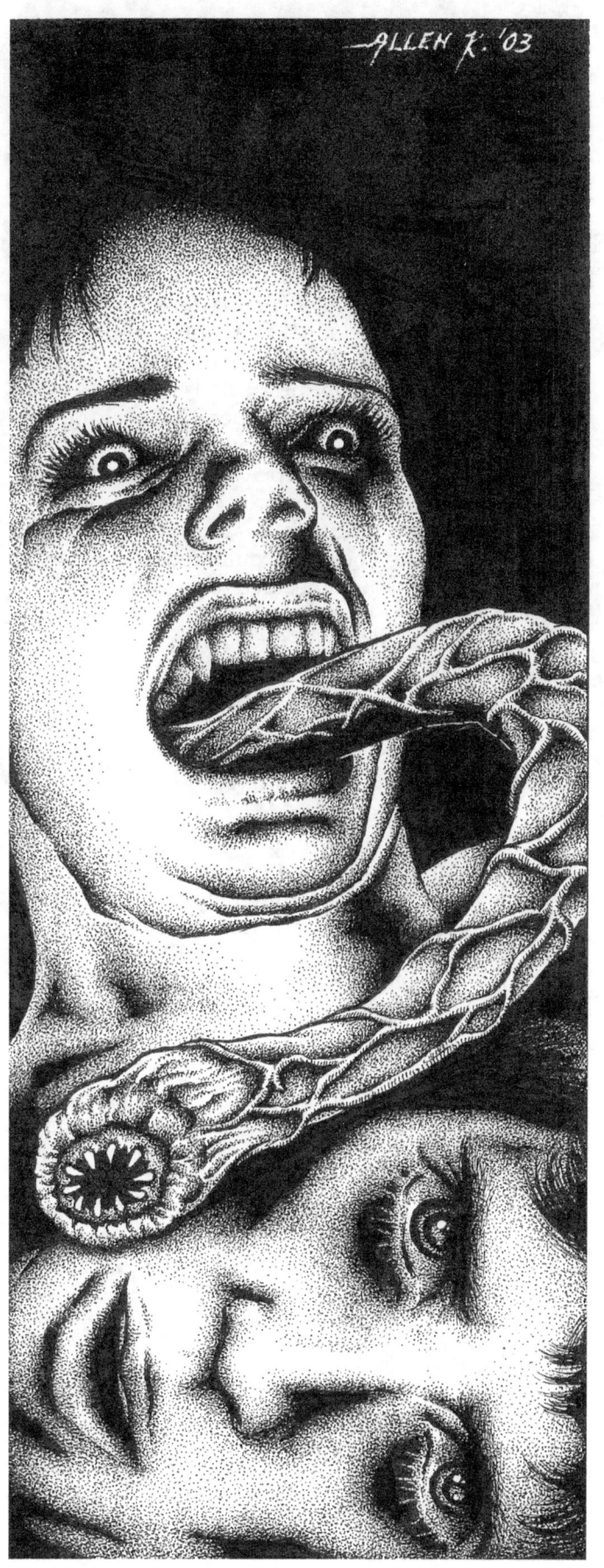

by Margaret L. Carter

"You watch your language, young man —" I bit off the end of the sentence. "Jeff, I'm trying to stop you from making a terrible mistake. I only want what's best for you." Never before had I felt more tempted to use mind control on him.

"You don't know a damn thing about what's best for me." He headed for the door.

"I know you've been sick for a couple of weeks — and don't try to tell me you're fine. I know it's that girl who's ruining your health."

A dull red flush crept over his face. "That does it; I've had it with you! You don't know what you're talking about. You've never even met her." Clutching the doorknob, he turned to glare at me. "Don't wait up tonight. I'll be spending the night at her house." He stalked out and slammed the door. A few seconds later, I heard his car roaring down the street. *Déjà vu* all over again.

I didn't bother trying to follow him, since he would cover several miles before I could get my car out of the driveway. Instead, I decided to go straight to the Manila Pearl. The manager there should have an address for Corazon.

Like most Europeans, the people of my homeland also prize garlic as a remedy against "demons." The way that plant affected me, I couldn't use it as a weapon. If Corazon turned out to be what I suspected, though, a common household ingredient harmless to me would disable her.

The thought of bursting into a strange house and catching my grown son in a compromising position made me squirm. But I couldn't stand aside and do nothing while Jeff deteriorated into an anemic zombie. I think I had some notion of disillusioning him by making Corazon show her true colors. And if that didn't work, I had no compunctions about getting rough with the creature.

At the restaurant I pulled right into the parking lot, which, again, was fairly empty. I didn't see Jeff's car; he must have gone straight to the woman's home. I took a stool at the bar and ordered a club soda from the same bartender who'd been serving the previous night. "Is Corazon off tonight?" I asked.

He blinked, apparently struggling with the ghost of a memory of our conversation the night before. "Yeah, she hasn't been in."

"I need to see her. Could I speak to the manager?"

"Speaking."

"Well — I really need to talk to Corazon. Could you give me her address?"

"No way, lady. Employee information's confidential." He turned his back to rearrange a row of bottles.

I stretched over the bar to tap his shoulder. He turned, his forehead creased in a frown of annoy-ance. When my eyes trapped his, his face went blank.

I trailed my fingertips down his arm to his hand. My touch made his heartbeat speed up. Hunger stirred in the pit of my stomach. I ordered it to settle down. "Tell me her address."

He recited it.

"Good," I said. "I'm leaving now. Forget you saw me."

In the car, I consulted the street map again. A few blocks of driving took me out of the commercial district along two-lane, badly-lit streets farther south into a shabby residential neighborhood. I inched past small houses with weedy yards, sagging front stoops, and peeling paint. The address I'd memorized proved to be a one-story cottage not much different from the others, except that it had no lights on. Jeff's car was parked in front of it.

I drove around the block, parked, then walked back to Corazon's place with my bulky purse hanging from one shoulder. The thought of breaking in worried me, since the noise might alert the woman. She had carelessly left the front door unlocked, though. *Probably in too big a hurry for dinner!*

Inside the dark living room, the air smelled like incense. Judging from the few lumps of deeper shadow I passed on the way to the hall, Corazon didn't go in for much furniture. A faint, wavering light beckoned me toward a bedroom on the left — one of two opposite each other, it appeared, with a bathroom at the end of the hall. I heard heavy breathing and a pair of heartbeats. The scent of blood cut through the incense fumes.

Neither person glanced up when I slipped into the bedroom. By the flame of a single candle on the dresser, I saw Jeff, with his eyes closed, stretched on a double bed next to an open window. He was still wearing his jeans. The woman crouched over him, her back to me. A sinuous tube the thickness of an electric cord stretched from her gaping mouth to his bare chest. *Just as I thought! Tiyanak!*

I groped in my purse and pulled out my "weapon," a box of salt. I took a couple of long strides toward the bed. "Get off my son, you —"

Corazon reared up and glared at me with a loud hiss. Her insectile tongue retracted an inch or two. Her eyes glowed crimson, like a wild animal's in a car's headlights.

"Get away from him," I snarled. Entranced by her spell, Jeff still didn't react.

She rolled her tongue back into her mouth and whispered, "Not likely. His blood has the most tantalizing flavor — human but not quite, spiced with something — extra. And he loves me."

"Enslaved by you, more like it! *Tiyanak!*" Distant

kin of ours, viciously predatory, making no attempt to live at peace with the day folk.

She stood up, smirked at me, and wiped a droplet of blood from her lips. "What do you plan to do about it, *danag?*"

I answered by flinging the entire contents of the salt box in her face. It stung her eyes, frosted her dark hair, and showered over her shoulders and breasts.

Corazon shrieked. Her hands curled into talons; her face shriveled into a harpy mask. Leathery wings sprouted from her back. Keening in pain, she leaped into the air and flung herself out the window.

Sometimes folk legends tell the truth.

I rushed to the bed and stared down at Jeff. Blood beaded from several fresh punctures. No time to moan over his condition; we had to get out before she recovered and came back.

I gripped Jeff's shoulders and gave him a gentle shake. His skin felt unnaturally cool. He didn't respond. "Oh, God, please wake up!" Realizing I was acting like a hysterical human female, I forced myself to calm down and extend my power into his mind. "Wake up, Jeff. We have to leave here."

His eyes opened. "Mom?"

"Listen to me, Jeff." This crisis was a clear exception to my rule against hypnotizing my own child. "Corazon is dangerous to you, and you to her. If you care for her, you will never see her again. This is for her own welfare. You understand?" Well, that wasn't strictly a lie. If she got near him again, I'd rip her head off, an outcome definitely not conducive to her welfare.

"Yeah." Jeff slurred the sound as if he were drunk or drugged.

"You will not return here or to the restaurant. You will not attempt to call or contact her in any way. And you will forget the details of your — love play. Is that clear?"

"Right." His eyes sagged shut; he began to sink back into a stupor.

"Wake up!" My sharp whisper jerked him into momentary alertness. "Stand up. We're leaving now. You have to walk to the car."

With my strength half dragging him, he got to his feet and made it out the door. On the way around the block, he muttered, "Mom? How'd you get here? Where we goin'?"

"Home. Where you'll get ten or twelve hours of sleep. And when you wake up, we'll have a nice long talk."

I realized that I'd made a mistake in keeping him ignorant of his ancestry for so long. If he'd known the truth about me, he might have been on guard against Corazon. And if that creature tasted a "not quite human" flavor in his blood, he might have more of my nature than I'd supposed. We had a lot to talk about.   Ω

FINAL VENGEANCE

The telephone announced the call
A wild staccato shout
That bounced a painting off the wall
And moved knickknacks about

The message so jarred Beverly
She fainted dead away
The husband killed so cleverly
Was coming home to stay

A voice she knew flowed from the phone
Announcing his return
But he was ash! Not flesh and bone!
She shook his empty urn

She armed herself with club and knife
She meant to do him harm
If her dead man came back to life
Then twice he'd buy the farm

He watched her scurry, locking doors
And sealing windows tight
He grinned to see her pacing floors
And spoiling for a fight

No, he would play with her for years
Before her curtain dropped
He'd sap her hopes and feed her fears
Until her life's blood stopped

The living Hell he gave his wife
Ceased with her final breath
Then his began with endless strife
She too survived her death

— **Alyn Miller**

by **Margaret L. Carter**   43

KADDISH

by Lisa Batya Feld

illustrated by Janet Aulisio

Anthony gripped the leathery neck and drank, ignoring the bristle and the acidic taste. Between hunger and anger he drained the man dry and flung him against the brick wall with a meaty **thunk**. The punctures in the man's neck sealed shut, leaving little evidence. "Pleasant dreams," Anthony growled, and headed home.

When he unlocked the door to the apartment, he could hear the stereo in the bedroom softly playing "Jesu Joy of Man's Desiring." The hint of prayer stung his ears and cramped his belly. He hung up his coat and went in.

Naomi was sitting up in bed this time, her large brown eyes full of as much quiet reproach as the music.

"I do have to eat," Anthony snapped.

"I'm sorry. I thought you'd be home later, or I wouldn't have played it. It's almost over." Her voice trembled, the rough quaver of age, not fear.

"It's all right. It doesn't bother me," he assured her.

"Who was it? Did you kill them?"

"Just a homeless man. I didn't kill him."

She frowned. "Please don't lie to me, Anthony."

Naomi's hair was as white as his, now, though her skin was speckled with age spots, unlike his own translucent flesh. She wore the dusky rose bed jacket he'd bought her in London; but though it had made her the picture of elegance at seventy-three, in the last few years she had fallen apart completely, her ravaged frame a parody of its former grace. The room still stank faintly of the accident she'd had on the way to the bathroom a few hours earlier, as well as other recent messes.

The last strains of the music ended, and Naomi shut it off with a soft flick of the remote. "I'm finding as I get older that my memories focus sharp on earlier times and leave the middle of my life on the shelf. My father loved classical music, even the Christian pieces. When I listen to that song I'm seven years old again, listening to the radio and curled on my father's chest, rising and falling with his breathing."

She was seven in the middle of the Great Depression, Anthony calculated. He'd loved the Depression. He wondered what Benito was doing now, seventy years later. Certainly not nursing his octogenarian lover through her last days.

Anthony and Benito used to fly up to roofs and pick off business men who had intended to jump, or finish off whole families before they froze to death in garrets. There was almost a sense of largess about it, dispensing death to the needy.

Naomi smiled, and her face glowed with it. It wasn't the smile of the young woman he'd fallen in love with fifty years ago. It was the smile of a mystic. It made him feel safe and terribly alone at the same time.

"What are you thinking about, Anthony?"

"If you'd let me change you when you were young, you wouldn't be in such pain now."

"That's not life," she said sharply. "How many times do we have to go through this? I couldn't live by killing things. I couldn't live a life that had no impetus for change, no growth, no natural conclusion."

He remembered her at thirty, cursing him for not being able to give her children; at forty, sick with jealousy and fear as her looks faded; at fifty, cursing him again for lost chances as the last trickle of blood ceased between her thighs; at seventy, when her hands trembled with the first traces of Parkinson's, when he'd begun looking for other food so as to save her strength. He'd seen the sadness grow in her eyes then, when he moved away, afraid and angry at her, giving her room to die. There was no romance in aging, despite her pretty words. In the end it came down to the fact that she couldn't bring herself to drink blood any more than she could eat pork. Lapsed or faithful, she was always a Jew. And he had to watch her die because of her picky eating habits.

"There is nothing *there*," he snarled. "I've killed hundreds of people and animals and in the end they're only *meat*. There's no heaven, no afterlife."

"You know what my synagogue looks like, yes?" she demanded.

He shrugged. "I've seen it, yes. The little brownstone on eighty-ninth street."

"What's the Rosh Hashanah service like?"

"How should I know?"

"You've seen it from the outside a hundred times," she said, "but you can't understand why I go until you go in yourself. I don't know what's on the other side. But I'm not going to throw away my one chance to find out."

"Don't you think if there was such a thing as a soul, if you lost it by becoming a vampire, I would have noticed the lack of it at one time or another?"

"Call the hospital," she said.

Blood poured from her nose, splashing on the bed jacket in a steady flow. Anthony stared at it, fascinated.

"Call the hospital!" she demanded, snapping him out of his reverie.

"Your grandmother has had another hemorrhage," Dr. Stewart said to Anthony. "We gave her another transfusion. But if she doesn't stay in the hospital where we can take care of her, she has a week left, maybe two."

"And if she stays?" said Anthony.

"A month, maybe more. She'll need to be on life support very soon. The nurses here can spare her some of the indignities she's suffered through the Parkinson's and the leukemia, and we can give her something for the pain."

"That's all right. I'm sure she'd want to be awake to enjoy the experience," Anthony snarled. "Fine. She stays here."

He pushed past the doctor into the semi-private room where Naomi rested and yanked the curtain shut. A plastic bag dripped vermilion into her veins. She had to live on the stuff anyway! What did it matter to her if it went into her mouth or into her arm?

Her eyes were closed, and he could see underneath the loose canvas of skin the face that had tilted back in pleasure when they made love, the fierce smile that had given way to helpless abandon.

She sensed him and opened her eyes. She lifted one trembling arm and he dove onto the bed, curling up in her arms and crying like a small child. "You stupid, stubborn —" he choked.

She kissed him softly, sweetly, "I'm sorry," she whispered.

He pulled away. "I should let you rest."

"Anthony, you can't control this. Or me."

He fled the room.

He took to the streets, filled at this hour only with delivery trucks, lovers stumbling home, and the oily smell of unsold fish. Anthony let his thoughts wander. The last thirty years had been lonely ones for both of them. They had to keep moving to avoid suspicion, which meant they couldn't maintain friendships for more than ten years. But Naomi couldn't make new friends either: new friends would question the presence of her grandson in a one bedroom apartment. And he had a hard time explaining to his fellow hunters why he stayed, year after year, with a woman who no longer looked the part of the vixen army nurse who had entranced him.

Not that they hadn't had a good run of it. What other man would have loved Naomi and helped her become a doctor in the middle of the fifties? She couldn't have done it if becoming a doctor meant living a loveless, solitary life, any more than she could have crammed herself into the rôle of a dutiful housewife just to avoid being alone. But however much she needed Anthony, he needed her more. Naomi steadied him, made him feel real. She made him live his life, pay attention to it, question it, instead of just wasting time between feedings. Anthony hadn't realized how empty he was until he started fighting Naomi, loving her.

Even though he could never explain Naomi to Benito, even though Naomi and Benito had hated each other from the moment Anthony introduced them, he couldn't help wishing Benito were here to crack a joke, start a killing spree, or swing around a lamppost singing opera. Most vampires, fiercely territorial, hunted alone. Between Benito and Naomi, Anthony had never been alone. He didn't think he had the stomach for it.

Damn her! She knew she could never have children so long as she was with him, she accommodated her hours to his anyway; what would she have lost by accepting his offer when she was twenty-five? Nothing but arthritis and chemotherapy. And now it was too late. Even if he changed her now, she'd remain a feeble old woman. She'd never have back her youth and beauty.

He could just leave her in the hospital. He should. It was terrible, inhuman, what she asked of him: to watch her die slowly, in pain, losing her dignity as her body betrayed her, even as her mind purified itself, readying itself for death, becoming alien to him. Once, last year, he had run away, and found that it was too late. Whether he was with her or a thousand miles away, she was dying in his mind's eye. If he didn't stay and love her until the conclusion, she would remain in limbo in his mind, always dying somewhere, never dead and buried.

He found himself retracing his steps, walking back to the hospital. He couldn't leave her there, prolong her death even further. He'd stay with her today, hidden from the sunlight, and take her home in the evening.

He'd expected her to be asleep; she dozed so often nowadays. But she watched him with a soft smile as he walked in. "My handsome man," she murmured, "I was just thinking of you."

"Yes?" he asked, coming to sit on the side of the bed.

"I was thinking of the night we met. I'd finally convinced the priest not to say the Last Rites for the Jewish soldiers, so I was staying up and saying Kaddish for — what was his name? — Howie Friedlander."

Anthony remembered. He'd been feeding on the dying in the dark corner of the ward, and the unexpected prayer had stabbed his guts and knocked him to the floor. "You were so angry, and you chased me out —"

"And you came back," she said, "So beautiful, so alien; I couldn't take my eyes off you." She grinned. "You demanded that I find you another source of food, since I insisted on acting as your judge and jury."

"And you offered yourself to me," said Anthony, "to keep me from killing the soldiers, you said, but you were so willing in my arms —"

"I loved you. I still do," she said.

"Something's upsetting you," he said, with the assurance of long experience.

"Nothing," she said.

"Please don't lie to me, Naomi."

"It hurts. And I'm afraid . . ."

Her hand was soft, textured with veins and fine bones. "And?" he asked.

"No . . ."

He knew that particular look of pain well. "You won't hurt me, whatever you have to say."

"My sister is dead, and my parents. All my relatives. There's no one left to say Kaddish for me. You don't just say it over the dead body, you say it every day for a year. I didn't realize how much it would hurt, the thought of dying with no one to sit Shiva, no one to say Kaddish."

"Are you sorry?" Anthony demanded. "Are you sorry for spending those years with me when you could have been making a family?"

She kissed him, long and slow, and he closed his eyes so he wouldn't have to look at her wrinkled face. "If I could to do it all over again," she said, "I wouldn't change those years."

She realized a second before he struck. "No! No, damn it!" She fought with the fragile strength of a bird, fluttering helplessly in his arms. She could have screamed for help; he could have broken her neck. He shushed her gently and his fangs slid from their sheaths and pierced her wrinkled, graceful neck.

She began the Kaddish, the prayer for the dead which fought him off even as it invited him in. "Yitgadal veyitkadash sh-shmei rabah —"

He could taste the blood of the stranger, the blood from the transfusion; but underneath he tasted the sweet flow of her that he'd almost forgotten. He cradled her head in one hand, holding her body with the other, and let the honey wine pour down his throat.

He held her long after the last tremors stopped, long after the last drop had sweetened his mouth, until the body was cold and stiff in his arms. Reluctantly, he eased her back onto the bed, kissed her lips, her forehead, as the pinpricks vanished from her throat. "Yitgadal —" the word wrenched pain through his bowels, made him gasp for air, but he kept going. "— veyitkadash shmei rabah, bialmah divrah chirutay viamlich malchutay —" he knew the prayer by heart and said it through to the last "amen."

Then he turned to the open window, and without a backwards glance, flew off into the night.   Ω

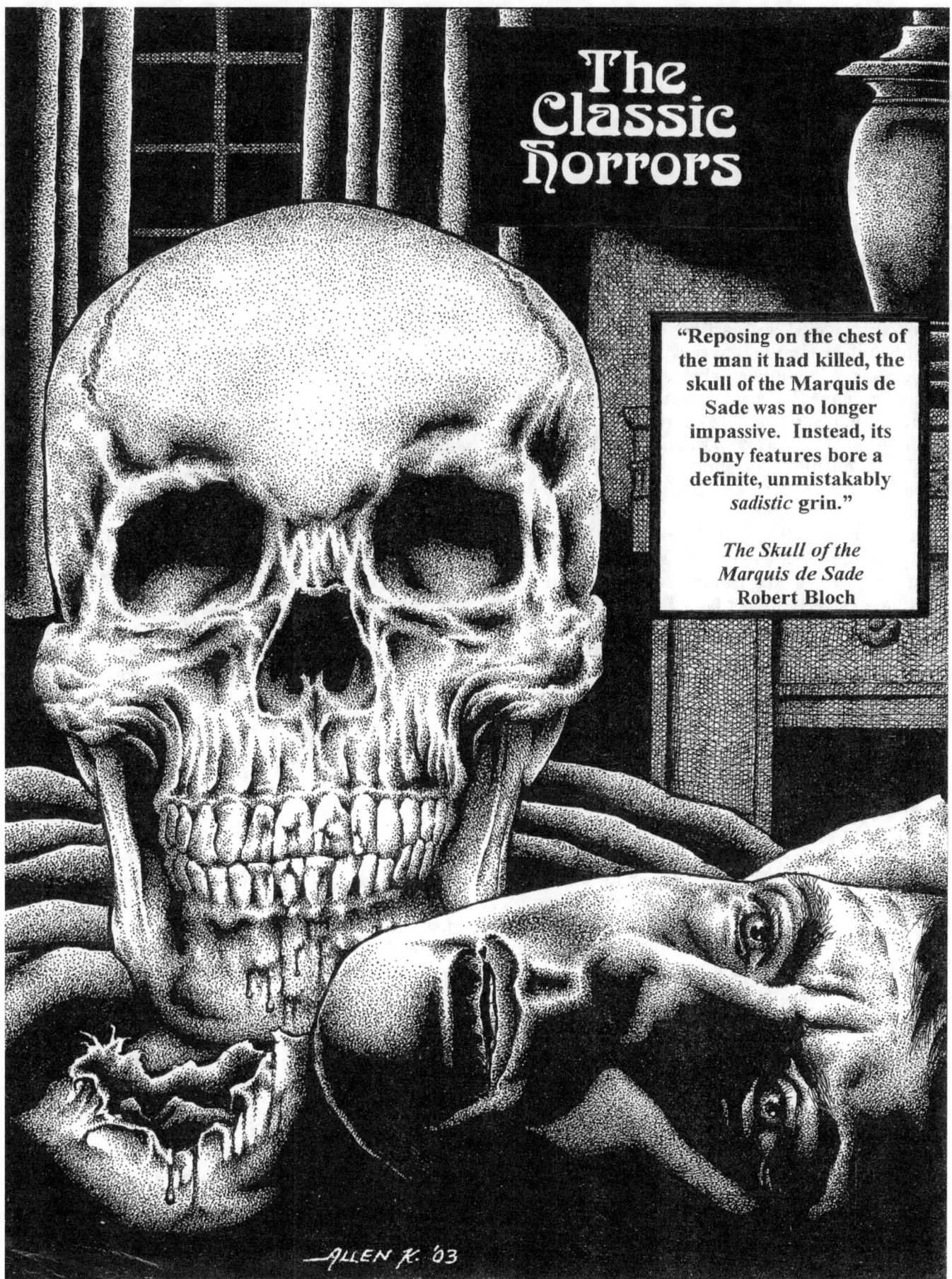

The Classic horrors

"Reposing on the chest of the man it had killed, the skull of the Marquis de Sade was no longer impassive. Instead, its bony features bore a definite, unmistakably *sadistic* grin."

The Skull of the Marquis de Sade
Robert Bloch

ALLEN K. '03

THE CLASSIC HORRORS

LEAVING THE SASQUATCH BUSINESS

by Marc Schuster

illustrated by Robert Cavanna

Beautiful how the old cars slow down — the Cadillacs, the Mustangs, the odd GTO pausing for a cherry-red moment of disbelief, tapping antique brakes with wide eyes as Dwight's hulking, hairy form disappears in the rearview, jaws clenched like a steam shovel, shoulders sloped forward for effect. The sun catches the chrome at all the right angles, casting long, jagged shadows across the highway as gold and brown leaves pirouette through sweet clouds of burning gasoline. A scathing memo handed down from above kills the impulse to look at his watch, and Dwight presses deep into the woods, blending into the foliage to the best of his ability. These are the days when the sun sinks low in the twilight sky. These are the days of magic and light.

Dwight's face twitches beneath a layer of black wool and rubber cement as he thinks about the tiny hairs sprouting up on his back, his real back, the back that sweats beneath the fuzzy monkey suit he's been wearing for the past three years, running up and down hillsides, darting from tree to tree, pounding his chest and howling at the moon for the benefit of passing motorists. The highway hums in the distance behind him, tollbooths lined up like military checkpoints at either end. Looking over his shoulder, Dwight peels a hairy sleeve away from his wrist and checks the time.

"Mommy! Mommy!" a thick German accent echoes through the woods, guttural and masculine. "Why is Bigfoot wearing a Timex?"

Dwight freezes, then laughs, cursing the German and covering the watch with his free hand. The man's name is Klaus. He works one of the night shifts and sometimes subs for Dwight in cases of illness, death in the family, or just plain boredom. His hominid is different from Dwight's in that Dwight plays the rôle with a sense of loping theatricality, infusing the primate with shy curiosity and playful abandon. Klaus, on the other hand, sees the rôle — the Yeti as he likes to call it — as more of a spectral figure, a looming presence haunting the fringes of perception, dwelling primarily in the realms of rumor and shadow, seldom stepping into the electric glare of passing traffic and society at large. At the very least, the philosophy gives him a chance to catch a few hours' sleep while he's on the job.

"You've got to be more careful," Klaus says, emerging from the shadows in a dark overcoat. Deep craters speckle his cheeks, and his eyes turn to thin slivers of glass when he smiles. "What if I were the Parks Commissioner?"

"Don't be silly, Klaus," Dwight says. "We both know there's no such thing as a Parks Commissioner."

Klaus throws a protective arm over Dwight's shoulder and says that he's just watching out for the boy. Leaves crackle like radio static beneath their feet. A large bird screams overhead. Are the woods getting tired, Dwight wonders, or is it just him?

"Illusions are fragile," Klaus says. "Like smoke. Like glass. If they see you checking your watch every five minutes, the whole act is shot to hell. You need to be like a child, Dwight. Innocent. Magical."

"I know." The dry forest whistles with a low October wind, and the pair descend a dark stairwell of tangled roots and misplaced logs. "I just don't think my heart's in it anymore."

"I see." Klaus turns a key in a heavy subterranean door and holds it open for Dwight. "You want to quit."

"Thank you, good sir," Dwight says, and they pass quietly through a dim tunnel, damp bricks dripping on either side, bare bulbs buzzing overhead. He hasn't thought about it in quite these terms yet: wanting to quit and all the negative connotations associated with the dirty word — failure, abandon, giving up and letting go. There were karate lessons, tennis lessons, piano lessons and paper routes. There were summer camp and math camp and Japanese in college. There were reasons and excuses, ailments and psychoses. And there were lectures on all sides about responsibility and commitment.

"I prefer not to think of it as quitting," Dwight says. He pulls at a pair of fuzzy rubber gloves and his hands begin to breathe again. "I'm moving on."

"Americans," Klaus laughs, opening a second door for Dwight. "A pleasantry for everything."

The lights in the office burn away the shadows and recast Dwight's world in harsh, blazing whites. His eyes adjust slowly, and he unzips the front of his hairy chest. A stack of paperwork waits on his desk, thick like a phone book, daunting, almost spiteful. A secretary named Evan adjusts his glasses and informs Dwight that Federal and State Regulations prevent him from undressing in areas other than those designated as Official Dressing and Undressing Areas.

"Sorry, Evan." Dwight scratches his bare chest and exposes his tonsils in a long, gaping yawn. "Won't happen again."

The trouble with Evan, Dwight figures, aside from his Abercrombie & Fitch good looks, is that he's something like the Secretary of the Interior's third cousin, which gives him the mistaken impression that he has a direct line to the President, which further causes him to spend his weekends drafting a lengthy report to his cousin documenting every transgression Dwight, Klaus, and the entire Operation Sasquatch team have made over the last year and a half. That Operation Sasquatch is a state-run program doesn't dull Evan's determination in the least, and the joke around the office is that he calls his mother every day at noon to tell her who's abusing their photocopy privileges and how many times he heard the F-word today.

"And I'm sure I don't need to remind you that forestry and traffic reports are due this Friday," Evan drones, wiping his glasses with a handkerchief. "Not that this information will phase you in the least, but I want it to go on record that I warned you."

Dwight grumbles something; and Klaus smiles his disarming Euro-smile, promising that the paperwork will be finished by morning. Evan folds his handkerchief, self-satisfied and smug. Klaus pushes open a third door, this one marked with a gold star and labeled DRESSING ROOM, and Dwight thanks him a third time.

"You know why the job's getting to you?" Klaus says, throwing his overcoat in the corner and taking a seat in front of a makeup table. He dabs the corners of his eyes with black paint and presses a gummed prosthetic to his forehead. "You take it too seriously."

Dwight sits down, studies his face in the mirror: sloped brow, fake fur, rubber nose. The image is framed with light bulbs. Dwight thinks of vaudeville and wonders how anyone can take this job seriously.

"Look at your paperwork," Klaus says. "You dread it because you read all the questions. 'To the best of your knowledge, how many motorists saw you today?' Ten? Fifteen? A hundred? Who cares? You're supposed to be a Yeti, a step or two up from the monkeys, and they expect you to count? Just do what I do and invent your own statistics. Life's too short for the real thing."

"It's not the paperwork, Klaus. And I'm not taking the job too seriously."

"What then?"

"I don't know." Dwight bares his teeth at the mirror and sees a stupid, clumsy oaf where a monster used to sit. He hasn't kissed a girl since college, and his gut's been creeping silently over his belt for the past year and a half. There was a time when he thought he could play the beast forever, ride his animal alter-ego into the grave, but the games are getting old. The magic is wearing thin. "What's the best thing that ever happened to you?"

"That's a tough one," Klaus says. He presses a set of plastic teeth into his mouth: yellow, brown and crooked, a distinct contrast to Dwight's white fangs. The department likes these minor incongruities, these subtle shifts in detail. They add to the primate mystique. "I've been around."

"My point exactly. I haven't been around. I haven't been anywhere. You want to know the best thing that ever happened to me? The *very* best thing? When I was in high school, a girl named Mary Brady told me I had nice eyes. It wasn't romantic or anything. We were in the school play together. She was a dancer, and I was one of those guys who lurks in the background and tries to look interested in whatever's happening on stage."

"Extras."

"Thanks. Anyway, Mary's got to be the prettiest girl in the whole school. I mean, you can tell she's a dancer by the way she walks, but here she is putting pancake on my face because the director figures guys can't do it themselves. Then it happens. She looks up at me, perfectly serious, and says, 'You know, Dwight, you have the most beautiful blue eyes.' Klaus, I'm telling you, I felt bulletproof, like I could fly to the moon and back. The most beautiful girl in the whole school tells me she likes my eyes, and you know what I did? Absolutely nothing. I walked right onto that stage and looked interested as hell at whatever was going on. A guy made a speech, I stroked my chin. A girl sang a song, I mopped my brow. Mary started dancing, and my eyes jumped out of my head. After that, she signed my yearbook, *Have a great summer!*"

"I see. You're quitting the best job in the world to search for some long-lost high school sweetheart who may or may not remember your name."

"I'm not quitting," Dwight says. "I'm moving on. And I definitely wouldn't call this the best job in the world."

"They let you dress like a monkey and dance on the side of the road, and you don't think it's the best job in the world?" Klaus slips a pair of hairy pants over his red longjohns and searches a closet for his monkey feet. "Now I know you're taking it too seriously."

"The thing is, Klaus, I don't want to go through life thinking the best thing that can happen to me is some girl I barely know tells me I have nice eyes."

"You do have nice eyes."

"You're missing my point entirely. If I stick with this job, the best I can possibly hope for is to catch a fleeting glimpse of an old Stingray motoring up the highway or to hide in the shrubs while some rich grease monkey changes a tire on his Deuce Coupe. Meanwhile I'm stuck driving a Hyundai to work and ogling other people's leather and chrome from afar."

"You and your cars."

"I can't help it," Dwight says. "It's the only language my dad and I both spoke."

Klaus lays a monkey's paw on Dwight's shoulder and wishes him luck. Lingering for a moment, he tries to recall a line of advice from his own father, but the sentiment gets lost in the translation. Settling for a quote from a John Wayne movie, he hunches his back and curls his lip to expose a row of rotten teeth, the transformation complete. Dwight thanks him for the advice, and Klaus lurches out of the room, grunting at Evan as they pass each other in the hallway. Yanking a stream of tissues from a half-empty box, Dwight begins to wipe the paint

from his eyes but stops when Evan pokes his needle nose into the room.

"Ornstein wants to see you," the skinny pencil-pusher says, folding his arms and lifting the corners of his mouth into a smug grin. Dwight eyes him in the dressing room mirror, bordering on jealousy. If not for the obvious personality flaws — lack of faith, paranoia, abject bitterness — Evan's wouldn't be a bad life to slip into once in a while. Then again, Mary Brady never told Evan that he had the most beautiful eyes in the world. At least, not to Dwight's knowledge.

"I'll be right there," Dwight says. "As soon as I get my face off."

"No," Evan tells him. "She wants to see you right now."

Evan says their boss's name as if it disgusts him, as if nothing pains him more than working for a woman who's spent her entire life moving from trailer park to trailer park, resting sometimes in a Motel 6 or stopping for fresh air at a KOA campground. Some people call her Mama Sasquatch, though she rarely goes into the field anymore. When Dwight calls her ma'am, she tells him to call her Millie and asks why he's still dressed like a monkey.

"My zipper got stuck," he tells her, silently cursing Evan's tedious sense of urgency.

A mannequin lurks in the corner of Millie's office wearing a tattered and considerably less detailed version of Dwight's costume — monochrome fur, sloppy stitching, visible buttons running up and down the chest. Back in the old days, before video cameras and digital enhancement, you could get away with a sham like that, but now it's an entirely different ball game. These days, if you want the public to believe in magic, you have to pay through the nose for detail and realism. Otherwise, you get caught in the freeze frame and the jig is up.

"You like the old girl, don't you?" Millie asks, swiveling around in her chair to admire the old getup. A dull, brown desk lamp offers the only light in the room. "She's a little on the shabby side but a real work of art if you compare her to the original. Would you believe I started this gig in nothing but a pair of old pajamas and my fuzzy bunny slippers?"

"I've heard rumors," Dwight says.

"My husband locked me out of the house. He wasn't a drinker or anything, just kind of dumb and tired all the time. He's dead now, but we got divorced long before that. He was my second husband."

Dwight rocks from side to side in his chair, studying the photographs on Millie's wall: Millie shaking hands with Jimmy Carter. Millie slapping Ronald Reagan on the back. Millie and the first George

LEAVING THE SASQUATCH BUSINESS

Bush smiling and waving at the camera with monkey paws. A framed letter from Bill Clinton commends her for single-handedly increasing the volume of traffic on our nation's highways. Trophies like these, Dwight imagines, drive Evan insane.

"So there I am on the side of the road, trying to flag down some help, and what do I see on the news that night but a report on a series of Bigfoot sightings in my area. I didn't think much of it at first, but then there's some grainy shots from a Super-8 movie camera, and there I am, plastered all over every TV set in town. In my pajamas, no less. Soon everyone's hitting the road and looking for this monster. I mean, it's a real shot in the arm for the whole area, right? T-shirts, bumper stickers, snow globes." She counts the burgeoning industries off on her fingers. "All of a sudden, I'm this pillar of society, and business is booming. Cars are lined up for miles up and down the interstate, paying their tolls to catch a glimpse of this mysterious window to the past, this missing link, this . . . What is it that Klaus calls her? This Yeti. So I can't just quit, can I? I have a duty to my constituents. Give the people what they want, right?"

"I'm sensing a moral to your story," Dwight says uneasily. He's read the abridged version in the company handbook: How Millie got the ball rolling, how she petitioned the state for funds, how the state came in and codified the entire operation in 1978. She's hinted in the past that she'll have to retire someday and hang up the old monkey suit for good, the inference being that if Dwight plays his cards right, he can work his way up to a cozy position in the front office.

"Moral?" she shrugs. "It's just a story."

"Evan said you wanted to see me about something?"

Millie smiles and offers Dwight a Tootsie Roll from a wicker basket on her desk.

"I could give up all my vices," she says, chewing. "And still I'd come back to sweets."

"Sweets," Dwight repeats, grinning stupidly. A wall of monitors glows behind him, flickering with images: key stretches of highway, the dark stairwell, the leaky tunnel. Millie sees everything, hears everything, probably knows everything that goes on in and around these woods, her woods. He unwraps his Tootsie Roll slowly, picking stray white fibers off the chocolate as Millie slips another into her mouth. They sit quietly, chewing, swallowing chocolate, each moving in vain to break the silence — faltering gestures toward an unnecessary reconciliation. In the old days, she'd have demanded an explanation; a letter, perhaps, to make the resignation official, but today is different. Coming and going is an occupation in itself.

"What do you think you'll do next?" Millie finally asks when prolonging the silence any further would border on the absurd.

"I don't know." Dwight pulls at the synthetic fibers glued to his chin. "I was thinking of getting my MBA. You never know, though. Maybe I'll take some time off. Travel. See the world. I've never been to Vegas."

Millie's eyes grow soft in the dim light. There are memories behind them, scenes from a life. Her smile is crooked and Dwight wonders if it betrays a hint of jealousy.

"You'll be a tough one to replace, Dwight," she says, and the days pass into each other, gold and brown and deep shades of red, each growing shorter than the last. Of course, there are the fond farewells, the moments of silence, the promises to keep in touch, to visit often. There are the documents to sign, the promises of confidentiality, the unspoken threats of legal action.

There are the lessons. Wearing Millie's old skins and tripping over his big feet as he makes mental notes for a report that will never see the light of day, Evan is a slow learner. But Dwight is patient with him. Detached and even relaxed as he drills the erstwhile pencil pusher on the basics of Sasquatchery: *What if a motorist pulls over? What if they have guns? What if you get caught?*

There's the farewell party, the cake, the hand-painted greeting card, and Klaus reads an ode to Dwight, rhyming his name with bright, night, and flight. There are slaps on the back and hearty guffaws. There are jokes. There are references to young monkeys wearing watches and old ones sleeping on the job. There's a glance at the clock and a reminder from Millie to get back to work. There are the final good-byes, and Klaus hobbles into the night. And in the end, there is Dwight, alone and upright, walking the dim corridor to his Hyundai, daydreaming of Mary Brady and wondering what comes next. Ω

KITTY LOSES HER FAITH

by Carrie Vaughn

illustrated by Russell Morgan

"This is Kitty Norville and you're listening to *The Midnight Hour,* the show that isn't afraid of the dark or the creatures who live there."

The calls were progressing nicely. I'd gotten the usual range, from disillusioned goth chicks to the furry and confused.

"My boyfriend *says* he's a vampire, but he likes drinking blood from my thigh instead of my neck. That's not right, is it?"

"I'm a werewolf trapped in a human body."

"Should I be suspicious if someone's Italian *and* they're allergic to garlic?"

The worst part about the supernatural underworld is not having anyone to talk to. It's a secret, dangerous world. Most join it against their wills through an act of violence: attacked by a werewolf, drained of blood by a vampire. Fear is powerful, even if you have five times the strength of a normal human, even if you possess virtual immortality. So much remains a mystery. If I can take away just a little of the mystery, maybe I can take away the fear.

As a werewolf, I know what I'm talking about.

I should have known by now not to get too comfortable. Every show, at least one call threw me for a loop.

Matt leaned on the doorjamb between the sound booth and studio. "Kitty? There's a live one on line three. Might be a crank, but she sounds like she's really in trouble. You want it?"

I could say no. This was my show after all. It would be a lot easier and better for everyone if I transferred her to a hotline. Too bad there wasn't a hotline for troubled vampires and werewolves.

I nodded, listening to my current caller's ornate commentary about miscegenation and purity of the species. Standard canned reactionary rhetoric.

"Uh-huh, thank you," I said. "Have you considered a career as a speechwriter for the Klan? Next caller, please."

"Oh, thank you! Thank you!" The woman was sobbing, her words unintelligible around the hysterics.

"Whoa, slow down there. Take a breath. Slow breaths. That's a girl. Estelle? Is this Estelle?"

She stopped hyperventilating somewhat, matching her breathing to my calm words. "Y-yes."

"Good. Estelle, can you tell me what's wrong?"

"They're after me. I'm hurt. They're coming after me. I need your help." Her words came faster and faster. My heartbeat speeded up along with them. Her voice lisped, like she held her mouth too close to the phone.

"Wait a minute. Explain your situation. Who's after you?"

She swallowed, loud enough to carry over the line. "Have you heard of Elijah Smith? The Church of the Pure Faith?"

I stood and started pacing. I'd heard of Elijah Smith and the Church of the Pure Faith. For the last three months I'd been trying to get an off-the-record phone interview with Smith. I'd talked to two dozen of his flunkies who gave me the run-around. I was almost ready to show up at his door and let him have at me just to learn something new. I so wanted to expose him for the charlatan I believed he was. Right now, the church caravan was parked some sixty miles away from the studio.

"Yes, I've heard of them."

"I left. I mean — I want to leave. I'm trying to leave."

"Oh. I mean — oh." I, who made my living by my voice, was speechless. No one had ever left the Church of the Pure Faith. None of Smith's followers had ever been willing to talk about him.

A year ago, an old revival-style tent sprang up in the middle of the night on the outskirts of Omaha, Nebraska. Posters appeared all over the bad parts of town, the known haunts of lycanthropes and vampires, advertising a cure. A cure based solely on faith and the intercession of a self-proclaimed holy man, Elijah Smith. There was no official documentation of what happened during that meeting. The tent disappeared by morning and a week later showed up in Wichita, Kansas. Then Pueblo, Colorado. Stories began circulating: the cure worked, this guy was for real, and the people he healed were so grateful, they didn't want to leave. A caravan of followers sprang up around that single tent.

Smith's congregation was known as the Church of the Pure Faith, "Pure faith will set you free" its motto. Some people, including me, screamed cult.

But no one who wasn't earnestly seeking a cure could get close. People who came looking for their friends, pack-mates, or clan-mates who had disappeared into that tent were threatened. Interventions were forcibly turned back.

I had so many questions: what was she? Had she gone looking for a cure? Did it work? What was Smith like? This was the interview I'd been waiting for.

"Okay, Estelle. Let me make sure I'm clear on this. You are — what, vampire? Lycanthrope?"

"Vampire."

"Right. And you went to the Church of the Pure Faith seeking a cure for vampirism. You met Elijah Smith. You — were you cured? Were you really cured?" What would I do if she said yes?

"I — I thought so. I mean, I thought I was. But not anymore."

"I'm confused."

"Yeah," she said, laughing weakly. "Me too."

Vampirism and lycanthropy are not medical conditions, so to speak. People have studied us, scanned us, dissected us, and while they've found definite characteristics distinguishing us from homo sapiens, they can't find their sources. They're not genetic, viral, bacterial, or even biological. That's part of what makes us so frightening — our origins are what science has been trying to deny for hundreds of years: the supernatural. If there were a way to cure vampirism and lycanthropy, it would probably come from the supernatural. In the case of a vampire, how else could one restore the bloodless undead to full-blooded life? Faith healing just might be the answer. That was the problem with trying to expose Smith as a fraud.

I didn't believe there was a cure. Someone would have found it by now.

Estelle sounded exhausted. How long had she been running? The night was half over. Did she have a safe place to spend the day? And why had she called *me?*

Witnesses. We were live on the air. Thousands of witnesses would hear her story. Smart. Now if only I could live up to her faith in me.

"Are you safe for the moment? Are you in a safe place or do you need to get out of there right now? Where are you?"

"I — I lost them, for now. I'm in a gas station, it's closed for the night. I'll be all right until dawn, if they don't find me before then."

"Where, Estelle? I want to send you help if I have to."

"I don't think I want to say where. They might be listening. They might follow you here."

This was going to be tough. One step at a time, though. I covered my mouthpiece with a hand and called to Matt. "Check caller ID, find out where she's calling from." Through the booth window I saw him nod. I went back to Estelle. "When you say they're after you, do you mean Smith? Do you mean his people? Do they want to hurt you?"

"Yes. Yes!"

"Huh. Some church. Why? Why don't people leave him?"

"They — they can't, Kitty. It's complicated. We're not supposed to talk about it."

Matt pressed a piece of paper against the booth window. *PAYPHONE — UNKNOWN*, it read.

"Estelle? Walk me through the cure. You saw a poster announcing a church meeting. You showed up at the tent. How long ago was this?"

She was breathing more calmly, but her voice still sounded tight, hushed, like she was afraid of being overheard. "Six months."

"What happened when you got there?"

"I — I arrived just after dark. There was a camp of tents, some RVs, campers and things. They were circled and roped off. There were guards. About eight of us gathered at a gate. There was a screening process. They patted us down for weapons, made sure none of us were reporters. Only the truly faithful ever get to see Smith. And — I wanted to believe. I really wanted to believe. One of the people they searched, I think he was a werewolf — they found a microphone or something on him, and they threw him out."

They threw out a werewolf. That took some doing. "People who've tried to break into the Church have met up with considerable force. Who works on the security detail?"

"His followers — everyone who lives and works in that caravan are believers."

"But they've gotta be tough. Whole werewolf packs have gone after him —"

"And they're going up against werewolves. And weretigers, and vampires — everything. It's fighting fire with fire, Kitty."

"So they're not really cured."

"Oh, but they are. I never saw them shape shift, not even during the full moon. The vampires — they walked in daylight!"

"But they retained their strength? They were still able to deal with a werewolf on equal terms?"

"I suppose so."

Interesting. "Go on."

"I was brought inside the main tent. It looked like a church service, an old fashioned revival, with the congregation gathered before a platform. A man on the platform called to me."

"This was Smith? What's he like?"

"He — he looks very normal." Of course. She probably wouldn't even be able to pick him out of a line-up. "I expected to be preached at, lectured with all the usual Biblical quotes about witches and evildoers that fundamentalists use to stir up prejudice. I didn't care, I would have sat through anything if it meant being cured. But he didn't. He spoke about the will to change. He asked me if I wanted to change, if I had the will to help him reach into my soul and retrieve my mortality, my life. Oh yes, I said. His words were so powerful. Then he set his hands on my head.

"It was real, Kitty. Oh, it was real! He touched my face, and a light filled me. Every sunrise I'd missed filled me. And the hunger — it faded. I didn't want blood anymore. My whole body surged, like my own blood returned. My skin flushed. I was mortal again, alive and breathing, like Lazarus. I really was! He showed me a cross and I touched it — and nothing happened. I didn't burn. He made me believe I could walk in the sun."

When Estelle first started talking, I thought I'd gotten someone who'd been disillusioned, who'd be ready to expose Smith's secrets and tell me exactly why he was a fake. But Estelle didn't talk like a disillusioned ex-follower. She still believed. She spoke like a believer who had lost her faith, or lost her belief in her own right to salvation.

I had to ask: "Could you, Estelle? Could you walk in the sun?"

"Yes," she said, her voice a whisper.

Goddamn it. A cure. I felt a tickle in my stomach, a piece of hope that felt a little like heartburn. A choice, an escape. I could have my old life back. If I wanted it.

There had to be a catch.

I kept my voice steady, attempting journalistic impartiality. "You stayed with him for six months. What did you do?"

"I traveled with the caravan. I appeared on stage and witnessed. I watched sunrises. Smith took care of me. He takes care of all of us."

"So you're cured. That's great. Why not leave? Why doesn't anyone ever go away and start a new life for themselves?"

"He's our leader. We're devoted to him. He saves us and we would die for him."

She was so earnest, it made me wonder if I was being set up. But I was close to something. Questions, more questions. "But you want to leave him now. Why?"

"It — it's so stifling. I could see the sun. But I couldn't leave him."

"Couldn't?"

"No — I couldn't. All I was, my new self, it was because of him. It was like . . . he made me."

Oh, my. "It sounds a little like a vampire clan. Devoted followers serving a Master who created them." For that matter it sounded like a werewolf pack, but I didn't want to go there.

"What?"

"I have a couple of questions for you, Estelle. Were you made a vampire against your will or were you turned voluntarily?"

"It — it wasn't against my will. I wanted it. It was 1936, Kitty. I was seventeen. I contracted polio. I was dead anyway, or horribly crippled at best, do you understand? My progenitor offered an escape. A cure. He said I was too charming to waste."

I developed a mental picture of her. She'd look young, painfully innocent even, with the clean looks and aura of allure that most vampires cultivated.

"When did you decide you didn't want to be a vampire anymore? What made you seek out Elijah Smith?"

"I had no freedom. Everything revolved around the Master. I couldn't do anything without him. What kind of life is that?"

"Unlife?"

"I had to get away."

If I were going to do the pop psychology bit on Estelle, I'd tell her she had a problem with commitment and accepting the consequences of her decisions. Always running away to look for a cure, and now she'd run to me.

"Tell me what happened."

"I was mortal now — I could do whatever I wanted, right? I could walk in broad daylight. I was assigned for screening duty at the front gate two nights ago. I lost myself in the crowd and never went back. I found a hiding place, an old barn I think. In the morning, I walked past the open door, through the sunlight — and I burned. The hunger returned. He — he withdrew his cure, his blessing. His grace."

"The cure didn't work."

"It did! But I had lost my faith."

"You burned. How badly are you hurt, Estelle?"

"I — I only lost half my face."

I closed my eyes. That pretty picture of Estelle I had made disintegrated, porcelain skin bubbling, blackening, turning to ash until bone could be seen underneath. She ducked back into shade, and because she was still a vampire, immortal, she survived.

"Estelle, one of the theories about Smith says that he has some sort of psychic power. It isn't a cure, but it shields people from some of the side effects of their natures — vulnerability to sunlight and the need for blood in the case of vampires, the need to shape shift in the case of lycanthropes. His followers must stay with him so he can maintain it. It's a kind of symbiotic relationship — he controls their violent natures and feeds off their power and attention. What do you think?"

"I don't know. I don't know anymore." She sniffed. Her voice was tight, and I understood now where her hushed lisp was coming from.

Matt came into the studio. "Kitty, there's a call for you on line four."

Four was my personal emergency line. Only a couple of people had the number. Ugh, it was probably Carl, alpha male of my pack, annoyingly overprotective.

"Can't it wait?"

"No. The guy threatened me pretty soundly." Matt shrugged unapologetically. He was mortal. Pure, one hundred percent vulnerable mortal, and he knew better than to mess with threats from the supernatural world. One of these days he was going to quit this gig, and I wouldn't be able to blame him.

"Estelle, hang on for just a minute. I'm still with you, but I have to take a break." I put her on hold, punched the line, and made sure it wasn't set to broadcast. The last thing I needed was Carl lecturing me on the air. "What?"

"Hello, Katherine," said an aristocratic male voice.

It wasn't Carl. Oh no. Only one other person beside my grandmother ever called me Katherine. My nose wrinkled. "Arturo. How the hell did you get this number?"

"I have ways."

Oh, please. I switched the phone over to live. "Hello, Arturo. You're on the air."

"Katherine," he said tightly. "I wish to speak to you privately."

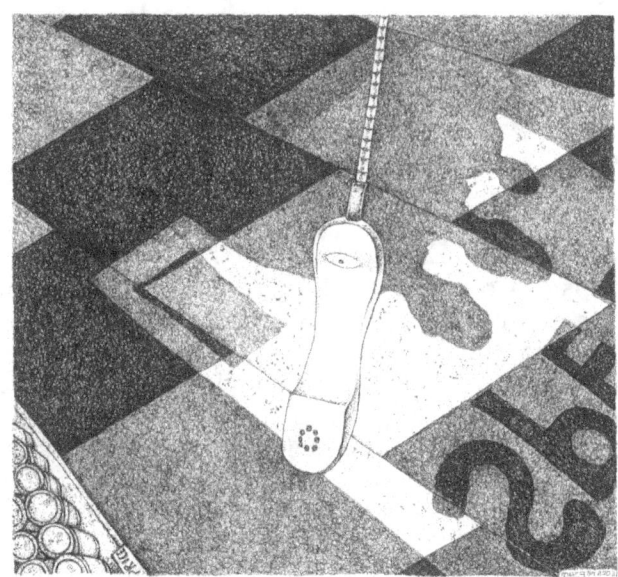

"You call me during the show, you talk to my listeners. That's the deal."

Arturo, the local Master vampire, tried to have me killed a couple months ago. Hired a werewolf hunter to do the hit on me while I was broadcasting. He thought the show stomped a little too heavily on his authority — he didn't like that some of his people were coming to me for advice and not him. The episode forced me to come out of the wolf-closet, as it were. Put my ratings through the roof. Maybe I should have thanked him.

"I do not appreciate being treated like your rabble —"

"What do you want, Arturo?"

He took a deep breath. "I want to talk to Estelle."

"Why?"

"She's one of mine."

Great. This was getting complicated. I covered the mike with my hand. "Matt, how does three way calling work again?"

A few seconds later, I had Estelle back on the line. "Estelle? You still there?"

"Yes." Her voice was trembling. She swallowed.

"Okay — I have Arturo on the other line —"

She groaned like I'd just staked her. "He'll kill me. He'll kill me for leaving him —"

"On the contrary, my dear. I want to take you home. You're hurt and need help. Tell me where you are."

Her breath hiccupped. She was crying. "I'm sorry, I'm so sorry —"

"It's far too late for that," he said, sounding tired.

I couldn't believe what I was about to say. "Estelle, I think you should listen to him. I don't know what I can do for you. Arturo can get you to a safe place."

"I don't believe him. I can't go back, I can't ever go back!"

"Estelle, please, tell me where you are," Arturo said.

"Kitty?" Estelle said, her voice small.

"Arturo — you promise you aren't going to hurt her?"

"Katherine, you're being harsh."

"Promise."

"Katherine. Estelle is mine. She is part of me. If she is destroyed, part of me is destroyed as well. I have an interest in protecting her. I promise."

Drama, tension, excitement! What a great set-up for a show! But at the moment I would have given my pelt to have the whiney goth chicks back.

"I'm going to break for station identification. When we return, I hope I'll have a wrap up for you on our sudden special broadcast of Elijah Smith: Exposed."

I switched the phone lines off the air and said, "All right, Estelle. It's up to you."

"Okay. Okay. Arturo, come get me. I'm at the Speedy Mart on 75th east of town."

Arturo's line clicked off.

"You okay, Estelle?" I asked.

"Yeah. Yes, I'm all right." She had stopped crying and seemed almost calm. The decision had been made. She could stop running, for a little while at least.

I had one more call to make — to the cavalry, just in case. I pulled a scrap of paper out of my contact book, got an outside line and dialed. After six rings, I almost hung up. Then,

"Yeah." Mobile phone static underlay the voice.

"Cormac?"

Cormac was a hit man who specialized in taking down vampires and werewolves. That he was still alive and able to use the plural on that meant he was good. He came after me, once. I talked him out of it. In fact, he owed me one now.

"Have you been listening to the show tonight?"

"Norville? Why would I listen to your show?"

So much for flattering myself on that score. "One of my callers is in trouble. Arturo says he'll help her, but I don't trust him. I want to make sure she doesn't get caught in a cross fire. Can you go help? Make sure nobody dies and stuff?"

"Arturo? Arturo is helping? She's a vampire, isn't she." It might have been a question, but he didn't make it sound like one.

I winced. "Yeah, actually."

"You're out of your mind."

"Yup. Look, chances are Arturo will get to Estelle first and the Church people won't even find her. But if the Church people do show up, they'll have some pretty hard-hitting supernaturals with them. You might get to shoot one."

"Whoa, slow down. Church?"

"Church of the Pure Faith."

"Hm. A buddy of mine was hired to go in there and never got through. I've been wanting to get a look at them."

"Here's your chance," I said brightly.

"Right. I'll check it out, but no promises."

"Good enough. Thanks, Cormac." I gave him the address. He grunted something like a sign-off.

Matt was signaling through the window. Time up. **ON AIR** light on. Okay. "We're back to *The Midnight Hour*. Estelle?"

"Kitty! A car just pulled up. It's not Arturo, I think it's people from the Church. They'll kill me, Kitty. We're not supposed to leave, they'll take me back and then — I've told you everything and now everybody knows —"

"Okay, Estelle. Stay down. Help's on the way."

Matt leaned in and didn't bother to muffle his voice for the mike this time. "Line four again."

Maybe it was Arturo checking in. Maybe I could warn him. He was Estelle's only chance to get out of there. "Yeah?"

"Kitty, do you need help?" said a gruff, accusatory voice.

Not Arturo. Carl. "I can't talk now, Carl."

I hung up on him. I'd catch hell for that later. He took his role as pack protector very seriously, and I was chronically prone to insubordination. We were going to kill each other one of these days.

Switched lines again, had to double check to make sure it was the right one. "Estelle? What's happening? Estelle?" Something rustled over the mouthpiece, then a banging noise like something falling. My heart dropped. "Estelle?"

"Yes. I'm hiding, but the phone cord won't go any further. I don't want to hang up, Kitty."

I didn't want her to hang up. A nasty little voice in my head whispered *ratings*. But the only way I was going to find out what happened was if she stayed on the line.

"Estelle, if you have to hang up, hang up, okay? The important thing is to get out of there in one piece."

"Thank you, Kitty," she said, her voice wet with tears. "Thank you for listening to me. No one's ever really listened to me before."

I hadn't done anything. I couldn't do anything. I was trapped behind the mike.

After that, I had to piece together events from what I was hearing. It was like listening to a badly directed radio drama. Tires squealed on asphalt. A car door slammed. Distant voices shouted. The phone slammed against something again: Estelle had dropped the handset. Running footsteps.

I paced, my hands itching to turn into claws and my legs itching to run. That happened when I got stressed. I wanted to Change and run. Run far, run fast, like Estelle had tried to do.

I called Cormac back.

"Yeah?"

"It's me. Are you there? What's happening?"

"Give me a break, it's only been a minute. Give me another five." He hung up.

Then on the other line, bells jingled as the door opened and closed. Footsteps moved slowly across a linoleum floor. I heard a scream. Then sobbing.

"Estelle. Won't you return to me? You can regain what you have lost. I'll even forgive this betrayal." A calm, reasonable voice echoed like it came from a TV in the next room. It sounded like a high school social studies teacher explaining a lurid rite of passage rit-

ual as if it were a recipe for mashed potatoes. A smooth voice, comforting, chilling. This voice spoke truth. Even over the phone, it was persuasive.

Elijah Smith, in his first public appearance.

"What are you?" Estelle said, as loud as she'd yet spoken but the words were still quiet, filled with tears. "What are you really?"

"Oh Estelle. Is it so hard for you to believe? Your struggle is most difficult of all. The ones who hate themselves, the monsters they are — their belief comes easy. But you, those like you — you love the monsters you have become, and that love is what you fear and hate. Your belief comes with great difficulty, because you don't really want to believe."

I sat down so heavily my chair rolled back a foot. The words tingled on my skin. He might have been talking to me, and he might have been right: I didn't believe in a cure. Was it because I didn't want to?

"A cure is supposed to be forever! Why can't I leave you?"

"Because I would hate to lose you. I love all my people. I need you, Estelle."

What was it Arturo had said: *she is part of me. If she is destroyed, part of me is destroyed as well.* Could Elijah Smith be some sort of vampire feeding on need, on his followers' powers?

If only I could get *him* to pick up the phone.

Yet again, I called Cormac.

"Yeah?"

"Has it been five minutes? At least keep the line open so I know what's happening."

"Jesus, Norville. Hang on. There's an SUV parked here. Three guys are standing guard in front of the building. I don't see weapons. They might be lycanthropes. They've got that animal pacing thing going, you know? Arturo's limo is parked around the corner. Lights off. Wait , here he comes. He's trying to

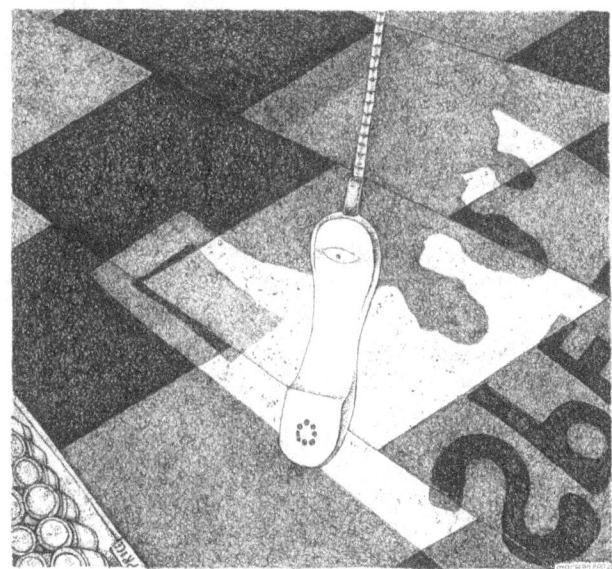

get in. I gotta go." I heard the safety on a gun click, then rapid footsteps.

I hated this. Everything was happening off my stage. I was blind and ignorant.

Then Cormac said, "Don't move. These are loaded with silver."

"You!" That was Arturo. "Why on Earth —"

"It's Norville's idea. Get your girl and get out of here before I change my mind. You, step aside. Let him through."

I had two lines open on a conference call. Two feeds of information culled from static and noise, all of it broadcasting. Outside, nothing. Cormac must have had something big trained on Smith's goons, because I didn't hear a grumble from them.

Then, from inside —

"Estelle? Time to come home. Walk with me." This voice was edgy, alluring. Arturo.

"Estelle —" Smith said.

"No. No no no!" Estelle's denial became shrill.

"Estelle." Two voices, ice and fire, equally compelling.

"Estelle, pick up the phone! Pick up the phone and talk to me, dammit!" I shouted futilely.

I wished I could talk to her. What would my voice do to the mix? What could I possibly say to her except: ignore them! Ignore us all! Follow what heart you have left, if any, and leave them.

She gave one more scream, different than the previous shrill scream of fear. This was defiant. Final. There was a crash. Something broke, maybe a set of shelves falling to the floor.

A pause grew, as painful and definitive as a blank page. Then,

"This is your fault," said Arturo, his voice rigid with anger. "You will pay."

"You are as much to blame," said Elijah Smith. "She killed herself. Anyone would agree with me. Her own hands are wrapped around that stake."

For a moment, I could feel the blood vessels in my ears, my lips, my cheeks. I felt hot enough to explode.

I could piece together the bits of sound I'd heard and guess what had happened. A piece of split wooden shelf, maybe a broken broom handle. Then it was just a matter of aiming, falling on top of it.

Goddamn it, my show had never gotten anyone killed before.

Arturo said, "What are you?"

"If you come to me as a supplicant, I will answer all your questions."

"How dare you —"

The door crashed open. "Everyone get out before I start shooting." That was Cormac, showing admirable restraint.

Quick, angry footsteps left the room, growing distant. Calm, slow footsteps followed. Then, nothing.

Cormac's voice burst through my silence, in stereo, coming though both lines now.

"Norville? Are you there? Talk to me, Norville."

My hands dug into the back of my chair. The upholstery ripped; the sound of tearing fabric startled me

When I looked, my fingers were thickening, claws growing. I hadn't even felt it. My arms were so tense, my hands gripping so hard, I hadn't felt the shift start.

I pushed away from the chair and shook my hands, then crossed my arms, pressing my hands under my elbows. Human now. Stay human, just a little longer.

"Norville!"

"Yes. I'm here."

"Did you get all that?"

"Yes. I got it all."

I hadn't even said 'thank you' to her. Thanks for the interview. I knew better than anyone how much courage it sometimes took just to open your mouth and talk.

"There's a body here. A girl. It's already going to dust. You know how they do."

"I should have done more for her."

"You did what you could."

A new sound in the background: police sirens. Just a minute too late.

Without a closing word, Cormac hung up, and I heard silence. Silence inside, silence out.

Silence on the radio meant death.

Matt said, "Kitty? Time's up. You can go thirty over if I cut out the public service announcements."

I gave a painful, silent chuckle. Public service my ass. I sat here every week pretending like I was helping people, but when it came to *really* helping someone —

I sat down, took a deep breath. I'd never left a show unfinished. All I had to do was open my mouth and talk. "Kitty here, trying to wrap up. Estelle found her last cure. It's not one I recommend.

"Vampires don't talk about their weaknesses as weaknesses. They talk about the price. Their vulnerability to sunlight, wooden stakes and crosses — it's the price they pay for their beauty, their invincibility. The thing about prices — some people always seem willing to pay, no matter how high. And some people are always trying to get out of paying at all. Thanks to Estelle, you now know what Elijah Smith and his Church offer, and you know the price. At least I could do that much for her. As little as it is. Until next week, this is Kitty Norville, voice of the night." Ω